"As well as being a ripping yarn that delivers on the sex and blood it promises, this is a wry and profound novel with disturbing resonance for the twenty-first century."

—*The Age* (Australia)

Praise for David Maine and *Fallen*

"Maine's storytelling is as human as it is divine."

—*Los Angeles Times Book Review*

"The book's power to rivet the reader approaches the miraculous."

—*The New York Times*

"Maine tells a fierce and visionary tale."

—*The Telegraph* (UK)

"With a modern novelist's art, acuity, and insistence on psychological realism, Maine manages what no religious teacher ever could and had me believing in the truth of these most archetypal of characters."

—*The Independent* (UK)

Also by David Maine

The Preservationist
Fallen

DAVID MAINE

The Book *of* Samson

ST. MARTIN'S GRIFFIN ✴ NEW YORK

THE BOOK OF SAMSON. Copyright © 2006 by David Maine. All rights reserved. Printed in the United States of America. No part of this book may be used or reproduced in any manner whatsoever without written permission except in the case of brief quotations embodied in critical articles or reviews. For information, address St. Martin's Press, 175 Fifth Avenue, New York, N.Y. 10010.

www.stmartins.com

Book design by Jonathan Bennett

Library of Congress Cataloging-in-Publication Data

Maine, David, 1963–
     The book of Samson / David Maine.
          p. cm.
     ISBN-13: 978-0-312-35338-4
     ISBN-10: 0-312-35338-3
     1. Samson (Biblical judge)—Fiction. 2. Dalila (Biblical figure)—Fiction. 3. Bible O.T.—History of Biblical events—Fiction. I. Title.

PS3613.A3495 B66 2006
813'.6—dc22

2006045803

First St. Martin's Griffin Edition: November 2007

P1

for my father

Author's Note

All character and place names are spelled as in the 1914 printing of the Douay Bible, translated by the English College at Rheims in 1582 and first published at Douay in 1609.

Samson

This is the story of my life and it's not a happy one. If you wish to read about me you're welcome to but if you're looking for something to give you hope & joy comfort & inspiration then you had best leave off here straightaway and go find something else. My life has an abundance of frustration and pain plus a fair bit of sex and lots of killing and broken bones but it's got precious little hope & joy comfort & inspiration.

It's got some women in it too plus a wife. Dalila is the one you may have heard of and a rare piece of work she was. You may think you know the story but believe me there's more.

It's an interesting question why anyone would seek hope & joy comfort & inspiration in a story in the first place. Something to think about. Maybe because there's precious little of it in life so we gather up as much as we can find and put it in our stories where we know where it is and it can't get out. But this story as I say isn't like that. It starts and ends with me here in chains and in between if anything it gets worse. Betrayal adultery and murder all figure in words writ large as if in fire against the nighttime sky. With the story not even done yet it might get more hopeless still before my days in this world are over.

In fact I'm sure it will.

To give an idea of the killing: I once left a wedding feast to go kill thirty men and then went back to the wedding which flowed on like wine unabated. This in response to a riddle and a wager. So you see I'm not joking when I say that murder is writ large in my life in words like fire against the nighttime sky. The thirty men's coats I removed from their stiffening bodies and then distributed to the wedding guests. Though normally prohibited from handling the bodies of the dead I was under some duress and consoled myself with thinking that they were so freshly killed that they were in fact not completely done with living as yet. Thus do we strike little bargains with ourselves and chip away at our integrity in the process.

The wedding where this took place was my own. Perhaps it conveys some idea of the nature of my in-laws that they took these new garments willingly enough and wore them happily afterward notwithstanding the rips bloodstains and other marks of wear.

I said this story begins in chains and so it does for I am in chains as I speak. They are iron and heavy and each link is the size of my hand and the thickness of my wrist. Mighty they are and in my prime they would have not held me but I'm no longer in my prime. As you might have guessed. The place of my enshacklement is a temple wondrously large which I've seen little of besides this sumptuous entertainment hall and the cells underground. In part this is because of the sorry state of my eyesight which is failing by the day. But I've seen enough to know that this hall alone is bigger than some villages I've walked through. At one end of it is a little platform like an altar or a stage and upon this platform I stand. Towering columns ring this hall: the largest being a pair at the far end and a second mighty pair behind me at the rear of the altar. So too is the looming statue of Dagon—the Philistines' so-called god which I will speak more of later. In the middle of the hall an enormous bonfire roars at all hours in a pit. I stand strung up at the edge of the altar with my arms spread in a T shape.

My legs are free to wander but alas there's nowhere for them to go. I spend my day shifting from one foot to the other trying to relieve the ache and for the most part failing.

Chains stretch from the shackles on my wrists to bolts driven into the columns. Maybe forty cubits in each direction. The bolts are as thick as a man and the columns couldn't be encircled even by ten men with their arms spread wide—and even these aren't as momentous as the columns at each end of the hall. Truly the palace is built on a scale beyond the understanding of simple men such as myself. I would say it is the work of the gods but that would be a blasphemy most foul as there is only One True God and I know that well. The difference between my people and the Philistines that surround me is that our God is the LORD of Abraham and Moses and Josue while the gods of the heretics are made of wood and they burn or stone and they sink or animal parts and they molder away over time. They are dull lifeless inanimate things. Dagon is the god of this temple and an imaginary creature nothing more. Half man half fish and pure nonsense as even a child could tell you but what can you expect from people who came swarming in their multitudes to Canaan in boats from across the sea?

At times the Philistines even worship the works of the One True God as being gods themselves so they pray to the thunder or the sun or various animals and engage in many other laughable superstitious practices.

I say laughable but admit I'm not laughing now.

This I will attest: that at the moment they have the upper hand but one day the LORD will give me back my hands to hold over them. As He has done so many times before. And when he does so those hands will not be empty but will contain a mighty sword or awesome club or at least a very heavy stone with which to smite them. And so I shall and they will break into small pieces and die. They will die. And I will laugh and dance as will my people. They will sing songs in praise of my deeds. And tell stories.

Those are stories which will have in them no dearth of hope & joy comfort & inspiration. Mark me well.

I fear I am rambling and not sticking to the point. I ask you to forgive me as this is a fault I'm prone to—which you'll see for yourself readily enough if you choose to attend my story for any length of time. The best thing for me to do now is start at the beginning for it is a story unlike any you have heard I have no doubt.

How I Entered the World

The manner of my birth was a sight wondrous to behold if one believes the stories as they are told and I see no reason to doubt them. Involving angels come to earth and signs in the heavens and so forth it must have quite overwhelmed my poor simple parents.

I use the words poor and simple in their poetic sense. My parents were not poor in things of the material world as my father had achieved some status in his native village of Dan and my mother's standing was of a commensurate level. Nor were they either of them simple in any sense of the word. But faced with the glory and grandeur and mystery of the One True God and witnessing the signs His angels made in the sky plain enough for even the blind to see—well how can anyone be but simple and poor when faced with such?

What happened was this. My mother lay back to birth me and out I came heralded at the same moment by a choir of angelic voices and the fiery wings of a bird outstretched across the firmament. Naturally I remember none of this. But I have heard the story so often I feel as though I was a witness to it rather than a participant however unwitting. With the bird's wingspan reaching from horizon to horizon all eyes were naturally fixed upon it not me nor my poor laboring mother either. And when at length the bird hurtled heavenwards to disappear into the Almighty's eternal reaches and the angelic host had roared itself hoarse—that is when my father and my aunts who were tending to my mother remembered to drop their gaze to where she lay sweating and straining against her matting already wet with birth-water and blood and perspiration.

I should mention that my mother was no longer a young woman and I as her firstborn was an unexpected gift in later life. Doubtless she wondered whether such heavenly displays were standard childbearing fare that heretofore she had somehow failed to observe.

As I say: Everyone looked at her and what did they behold? These midwives and attendants and sisters of my mother as well as my father who had sired me? They beheld my mother and then they saw her offspring. A pink-smeared but strangely placid infant sitting upright between my mother's glistening thighs which as anyone will tell you is not normal for a child of only a few moments. What's more I had a thick tangle of black curly hair even as I have now but slick with the fluid of my mother's belly. Most strangely of all perhaps was the fact that I grasped in my hand a stone of not inconsiderable weight. It was well and truly a rock—not just a wad of hard earth or ossified dung but a gray chunk of granite shot through with silver threads of mica and quartz. And with all these people watching me—so the story goes—I sat up and looked right back at them and the silence stretched between us like a length of gut pulled taut till it hums. And then when the silence had stretched as far as it could and the angels were gone and the wings of flame had vanished and my mother's breathing had settled into a rhythm fast and shallow—that's when I held that stone aloft. Held it overhead in one chubby infant's arm.

And crushed it one-handed till the powder sifted gray between my fingers still sticky with the drying grease of my mother's womb.

Seeing this my father raised his hands and said—Verily on this day has the Lord sent unto us a champion. Or words to that effect. This story has been told and retold so many times since the events took place that doubtless my father's utterance has grown more refined over the years. I could be convinced with little trouble—knowing the manner of man he was—that at the time his actual words were more akin to—Heaven save us all from this demon! or even something coarser such as—Fuck me brother! which was all in all his favorite expression of wonder or surprise.

But anyway. Whatever he said or didn't say I can't vouch for. The story was soon enough about that I was the champion sent to deliver the people. My people the Israelites. All that was wanted was the opportunity as well as of course a few quiet years for me to grow up.

Some History

It has been written elsewhere but maybe you haven't read it so here I will say it again in brief:

First came Adam and Eve whom you may have heard of and their children. One of those was Seth whose son Enos begat a son named Cainan who later begat a son named Melaleel and so on for quite some while. I assume there were women involved in all this begetting but little mention is made of them. Whether by choice or oversight I couldn't say. However I stand by my assertion as I have seen many wondrous things in my life but I've yet to see an infant born of a man whether out of his stomach or mouth or anus or any other unlikely place.

While this activity was going on there was also the other ordinary intercourse of human existence which is to say: plowing & planting birthing & dying building & destroying fucking & fighting. Especially these last two. The story as I understand it is that the Lord made all the animals and then He made human beings but I can't see as that things changed terribly much from the morning of the sixth day to the afternoon. By which I mean that if you looked at the history of human beings since the days of the Garden and then at another history—that of pigs leeches and wolves—you would not discover any extraordinary difference.

But I'm not sticking to the point which I warned you is a habit with me. I can get distracted by one thing or another and as likely as not that thing will be a pretty face or the swelling of a woman's backside. Such has been the case more than once and I'm sure you're eager to hear it all and so you shall but first other things must be told. So bite back your impatience for I promise to bring to you more than one swelling backside before my sorry tale is done.

History is what I will discuss for now. What you must understand is that the land where my people the Israelites lived after we descended from Abraham and Isaac and Jacob was at the time of my birth possessed by us no longer. Or not solely. There are many reasons for this but the main one is that my people had chosen to turn their backs on the One True God and had fallen into immoral and idolatrous ways which is something they seem to do with numbing regularity. Ever since Moses led them forth from the land of Pharaoh they have shown themselves remarkably unreliable in this regard—to the point where I have wondered more than once whether the One True God hasn't felt a touch of doubt over whether the people He has chosen were in fact the right people after all.

So then. Before I was born was one of those times when idols ruled our hearts and minds and the affections of my tribe were easily swayed by things of little value. And at that time we fell under the rule of the Philistines and all was not well for us. But I think giving this little history now has only led to the need for more.

I know you're hungry for sex and blood. Just a little longer I promise.

The Philistines

Imagine a small closed hut with only one door and then put a rat inside and stop up the door and what will happen? The rat will not be happy but given time it will perhaps grow placid enough. This is especially true if you make the effort to provide it adequate water and food and a place to deposit its waste and—if you feel generous—a she-rat for it to void its loins into. Supposing this hut is large enough then over time even the most ill-tempered of rats might grow to learn serenity and peace. I'm not saying it's certain to happen but it might.

Suppose however that into this small enclosed hut several more large rats or even rat clans are introduced. The outcome would be predictable. Although in the long run maybe all the animals would learn to coexist in a certain hierarchy of power understood by themselves alone and in constant flux you would have heavy work of it in the meantime: cleaning up dead bodies torn bits of fur and congealing puddles of blood.

Well this is close enough to what happened in the land called Canaan which is the land of my people the descendants of Isaac and Jacob. We lived there for a time before being taken away to the land of Pharaoh for 430 years which is plenty long enough for things to change and when Moses led us back lo! there were strangers in the place we had left. These were the Philistines who apparently had arrived on boats while our attention was otherwise occupied with making strawless bricks and so forth. These new arrivals were reluctant to depart so the only thing to do was of course to fire their homes

& salt their fields rape their women & murder their sons which we duly did. Before you call us rash or unthinking remember that we acted thus because the LORD commanded it so think hard a moment about whether you would have the nerve to look the One True God in the eye and call Him rash or unthinking.

So then. We didn't worry overly much about distinguishing between Canaanite and Philistine although it must be said that the Philistines arrived after we did ourselves while the Canaanites had occupied this land all along. Anyway there was little enough difference since—going back to my example—the hut was small and there was by now an overabundance of rats.

My people trusted in the LORD to sort out this confusion and sort it out He did.

Josue led the charge and soon the air was sweet with the smoke of burning bodies and ruined lives. Along with many other wondrous signs I'm sure you know such as the angels sounding their trumpets and the walls of Jericho tumbling into ruin and the sun halting in its journey across the sky so as to give us the extra time we needed to finish the slaughter. And I defy any man to think on these things and take them to heart and conclude anything other than the obvious which is that my people the Israelites are favored by the LORD above all other men.

However this happy turn of events didn't last long for it led to no end of problems as the Philistines took it upon themselves to ignore this obvious conclusion. Instead they chose to fire our villages & salt our fields rape our daughters & murder our sons in return. This of course couldn't be tolerated and so we retaliated and so they retaliated and thus it has lasted for many years right up to this day—an endless back-and-forth between the two nations with each striving for ascendancy but neither keeping it for long. There are many stories to tell from this conflict but I haven't the strength to tell them now. Suffice it to say that at length we reached an uneasy equilibrium with both sides pecking at each other like crows at a corpse while avoiding all-out war. But from time to time one side or the other gains in strength and then it is hard going indeed for the others.

Some forty years before my birth the Philistines had seized the upper hand and as a result controlled much of the area gifted to our forefathers by the One True God. Now however the LORD did nothing to help us. As I mentioned this was because most of our elders were busy prostrating themselves before large statues of half-men-half-fish or else pigs and roosters fashioned from precious metals or else onyx carvings of large-breasted naked women. Or in at least one case that I have heard it was the large-breasted naked woman herself who was actually being worshipped and not just on bended knee either. Sundry other meaningless blasphemies took place with monotonous regularity as well—many of which were derived from the practices of the heathen Philistines in the first place. So then does sin magnify and multiply itself in a manner truly diabolical.

During this time certain clear-sighted individuals took it upon themselves to devote their lives to the LORD by becoming Nazirites. They dedicated their lives to giving glory to the One True God in every way including self-discipline as well as the elimination of the Canaanites who were the native heathens plaguing this land like pox. But Canaanites as I explained before weren't the same as Philistines who were a different pox. It's all a bit complicated I know.

There were as well sundry other tribes despoiling the land such as the Ammonite nomads and the desert-dwelling Edomites. These last were descended from Jacob's twin Esau. Both of course were sons of Isaac. Jacob—also called Israel— begat the Israelites: Esau was cheated of his inheritance and his progeny have been in conflict with us off and on ever since. So those who say that Israelites and Edomites are naught but feuding cousins speak truly.

Anyway in the tale of my life it's the Philistines who figure most importantly.

Such was the situation in the land when I was born but before that happened my parents were first gifted with their remarkable visions. I should have told this earlier but got distracted with all this history that pushes down upon my people like a heap of millstones upon our backs.

A Most Extraordinary Visitation

My father Manue and my mother Sala had reached that point in their lives when they had resigned themselves to an old age of childlessness. This is not to say that they were decrepit already but rather that they had gone past the first flush of youth when most couples bear the bulk of their offspring and they had none. Whether this preyed on their minds unduly I can't say but I will acknowledge that for most people life is hard and old age is harder: hardest of all is an old age absent of the voices and laughter of one's progeny. Or so I have observed but cannot aver with certainty not being old myself as yet nor ever likely to be if I'm to judge by my current straits. But I get ahead of myself.

The day my mother was approached by the angel was an ordinary day in spring like any other. It was sunny enough to be warm without scorching and dry enough to be comfortable for sitting and staring at the river that ran along our village boundary. This sitting and musing was a habit Sala my mother was prone to all her life. Others in her family mocked her for it but gently and as I grew older and broader the mockery grew gentler still. What she may have thought about so much has been lost to history but from what I know of my mother it would have been topics as various as the wheeling mystery of the seasons or the secret destinations of the birds overhead or the long ropey tangled muddle of time itself.

So when she heard the voice saying her name she was most likely distracted and looked up with the little frown that accompanied her face when interrupted in some half-formed thought. And then she said—What is it?

And then she was looking at the angel.

Now later when telling this story she would always break off and not answer my questions when I asked—What did it look like? Tell me! and she would press her lips and shrug and say— Tell you what? He looked like a man but not like a man. I didn't even realize he was an angel till later. At the time I thought he was only a strange man who frightened me.

—Strange how? I would demand.—Frighten you why?

—Leave this she would say.

I will let you imagine for yourself how frustrating this felt for me as a child to have a mother visited by an angel of the

LORD but who had no further word to say on the subject.

Or at least not many words. There were clues in small pieces that built up over time into a picture like a mosaic. Her favorite comment was to say—It was awful. A funny description for an angel but I have none better. Usually her eyes screwed tight at the memory and once she said something about an unnatural flame. A dark fire I think it was. Twice or thrice more she mentioned light but then also shadows so take your pick. And to my father she said that the angel's face was difficult to look upon directly. Later in life she took to saying she had fainted from the shock and remembered nothing but no one believed this obvious falsehood designed as it was to relieve her from further storytelling.

Whatever the angel looked like—fiery or shadowy awful or divine—what remains indisputable is what he told my mother. Which was:—You are to have a child.

—How can this be? she asked him.—I am barren.

Remember that Sala my mother did not know then that she spoke to an angel.

And the angel said—Doubt not the power of the Lord.

And my mother had no answer as I doubt many of us would have an answer. So to fill the silence she asked—A son or a daughter?

—A son said the angel.—Now listen. You must abstain from wine and strong drink and you must eat no unclean flesh. For he shall be a Nazirite. Do you understand what this means?

My mother frowned and bit her lip. Or so I believe because she always did so at this point in the story.—Something about wine she said.—Wine and hair.

—Neither knife nor razor shall ever touch his head. Strong

drink he shall forswear and he is forbidden from all contact with the dead. Is this clear?

My mother said—Mm-hm. Probably she was thinking that keeping her child away from strong drink and dead bodies would be simple enough. Little did she know!

At this the angel took its leave from Sala my mother. And maybe she really did faint at that point because for the remainder of her life she maintained that she never saw it turn and walk away.

The Second Visit

Sala went to Manue my father and said—I met a godly man who told me that I am to have a son. And my father squinted at my mother who was shapely enough after a childless life and prone to musing and dreaminess and my father said:—Uh huh.

My father was a man who tried a little of everything and a lot of a few things in his attempt to control the course of his life. He kept some sheep and raised chickens. He traded eggs for wheat and let some chickpeas grow wild on our land. He let the potters dig clay from our river in exchange for a portion of their finished work and split firewood for the widows who repaid him with lengths of linen. Pots and cloth both he traded to merchant caravans passing south towards the Philistine cities of Timnah and Zorah. On occasion he would lend money and he wasn't averse to doing business with any honest man whether Israelite or Philistine Ammonite or Edomite Canaanite or whatever other ite might be willing. His reward for this openness was a fair degree of success and only occasional ugliness and difficulty. He taught himself smithing and could mend a pot or sharpen a sword as well as most men by which I mean it would last a season before cracking again. He respected my mother's dreaminess because he didn't have a single featherweight of it himself so he suspected it must indicate a nature both frail and profound. But he had his doubts about it too. Sometimes he viewed my mother as a semi-celestial being herself like some hollow-boned migratory bird brought unjustly to earth. And so he had the habit of not quite believing that she could negotiate this worldly existence of men & brutes desire & unkindness. So when my mother gave him the news his reaction was one of reserve. His first answer was—Uh huh and his second which followed only a few heartbeats later was:—This godly man of yours wasn't trying to undress you at the time was he?

At which my mother blinked and stared and then blinked again before laughing. Her laugh was something like a bulbul's trill and it delighted all who heard it. My father's own laugh was akin to two rocks being smacked together.

Manue left her for the time being and returned to his smithy where Sala rushed to find him later that same afternoon.— He's back! she cried.—He's come back! Come see!

Manue followed his wife. And who should he find but the same shadow-fiery figure who had appeared earlier to Sala. My father being the type of man he was was better able to describe this creature as having eyes like glass and breath like jasmine while waves of heat rolled from its body. It's worth noting however that over the years these details grew more elaborate with each retelling such that even I—who miss much— noticed this.

My father said—You're the one who spoke to my wife?
—I am.
—What do you call yourself then?
—Ask me not this thing. My name is not important.

From anyone else this would have been an unbearable provocation for my father was a plainspoken man and expected no less from strangers on his land. But this one had such an air of weirdness and calm to him—not to mention eyes like glass and breath of jasmine—that my father felt no anger. He was you'll remember still ignorant that he was speaking to an angel of the One True God. A seer maybe or even a prophet. But an angel?

Manue said—I understand you've got some instructions for our child. If it's true that a child we are to have.

—You may be sure of that said the stranger.—He will be famous throughout the land and for all time and his deeds shall be many and glorious.

My father probably scratched the back of his neck for such was his habit when weighing the likelihood of a thing.—Well that's great he said.—So what would you have the boy do? Or not do?

And the stranger said—Your wife knows. Avoid strong drink and unclean food. For it is commanded that he shall be a Nazirite and if you obey your child will be known for mighty works indeed. You must ensure that he is brought before the priests of the tabernacle and consecrated in due course. If you fail in this then much else will be lost and you shall carry the blame.

My father wasn't accustomed to being issued commands—least of all about things that hadn't happened yet and by people he didn't know. But this figure—seer or prophet or whatever he was—carried with him an undeniable oddness. So Manue said something like—Well now. And they all three of them stood like that for a time and perhaps my father wondered at this man's queer bluntness and perhaps my mother's eye followed the drunken loops of a butterfly as it meandered around the stranger's ears or her own. Then my father remembered his manners and said—Come eat with us then. For if you're right we should celebrate.

But the stranger only shook his head and said—A burnt offering unto the LORD would please me more.

My father probably grunted at this partly in exasperation but also in agreement. For who could disagree? In short order he assembled a pile of dry slash timber and twigs and a few stout logs and set the whole heap ablaze. And when the flames were at their highest he took the nearest kid goat that was to hand and sliced its throat and tossed it still kicking to smolder upon the pile and then scattered the contents of the wine jug onto the flames for my father was never a man to do anything only partway. And the kid's burning hair mixed with the sweet odor of sizzling wine and the hiss of damp slash sent a great fist of black and gray up into the sky towards God.

It was while my parents stood watching this smoke boil up that they noticed something else in amidst it passing in and out of their sight like a dream half-left in the morning. And then with a gasp they realized that something uncanny was happening: their mysterious visitor was ascending towards God along with the smoke. At that moment they both understood that that which had been but lately standing speaking to them was no human being but really a manifestation of the divine. Or an angel as they referred to it in later life.

They gawked around themselves. They were alone just the two of them. The stranger had gone.

—Well that's it then said Manue my father.—Now we shall surely die.

—Why is that? asked my mother with most likely a dreamy smile still on her face as she tried to squint past the smoke that summoned tears.

—We have seen God. And none can live after that.

Sala my mother considered this but wasn't convinced. She said—First of all I'm not a bit certain that was God. It looked sort of puny to be God don't you think?

—For God's sake watch your tongue groaned my father.

—And secondly if God had half a mind to kill us He could've done so long since. He wouldn't have waited for us to make a holocaust and offerings and then told us those things about our—And here her voice caught a little—our son.

Manue had no answer to this. Maybe he went back to his workshop then or maybe he took his wife in his arms. I was never told. Maybe they stood trembling in awe at what they had lately witnessed or even quietly wept. But I don't think so. My father was a man of strong appetites quick temper and common sense. My mother was prone to introspection and making the best of things. Neither gave over easily to tears.

The World Growing Dim

It's strange. As I stand here in chains with my eyesight failing from one morning to the next you'd think I would take refuge in memory. And the older the better: distant pictures of a happy childhood far from this place of tribulation. But no. Such memories I can barely recall.

What fill my mind are the more recent episodes from my life that led me down the path with this as its ending point. My battles with the Canaanites and Philistines and temptations by the harlots and of course my own thrice-damned stupidity. Soon you'll hear it all and then you can make up your own mind about her. About Dalila.

Did I say I'm losing my eyesight? That I'm going blind? I lied. I went blind the moment I looked at her.

The Priest

—Good morning Nazirite! chirps the voice at my ear.

I ignore it as best I can but it's never gone for long before it comes bouncing back. Now it says—For I would characterize any morning that sees you in shackles as ahh a *good* morning indeed.

It is one of the so-called priests of this cursed temple. His name is Meth or Menth or some such and he has formed a special enmity towards me. I don't know why. He clings to me like a leech except worse because a leech once flicked away will curl up and ignore you. But this creature sucks my blood each morning only to return at midday for more.

Doubtless the Philistines would say that I'm unfair to the wretch and so biased that my word cannot be taken for simple truth. To which I would answer that the Philistines are themselves hardly free of bias and for proof of this you need look no further than the manacles that clamp my wrists.

—How goes it with you Nazirite? the priest asks now with all false courtesy and brotherly concern.—Made it through another night I see. Good good. We don't exactly want you comfortable do we? But we don't want you expiring on us either.

—No danger of that I growl. Then to needle him I add—Is this how your Dagon slays his enemies? Through boredom? For that's the likeliest outcome for me.

His laughter is brief.—Oh you shall have worse than that to contend with never fear.

—I don't fear anything I said.

—Feeling brave are we? Meth or Menth pushes his face close up against mine and even my poor eyesight can make out his flinty eyes & pocked flesh weak chin & thin lips. He says—Feeling as brave as when you were hacking up those poor boys in Ascalon?

—You know nothing of Ascalon I grunt.

—Oh I know plenty he says.—Believe me. And Meth or Menth leans closer than ever—I can taste his acrid breath in my lungs. His nose cleaves my vision like a scythe and for a moment I wonder if he plans to kiss me. Instead he says:—I had family there. Understand Nazirite? I said *had* not *have.*

—I understand I say.

—I hope you do he whispers. Suddenly his voice has lost all semblance of warmth or concern:—Trust me you shall die in this place but it shan't be boredom that kills you.

With that he straightens quickly—as if he has said too much—and is gone.

Don't worry. I will tell you about Ascalon when the time comes.

An Incident from My Childhood

My father did as he was told. On the sixth day after my birth he brought me to the priests of the tabernacle and dedicated me as a Nazirite. This meant that I was to live my life without touching dead bodies strong drink or unclean meat. The unclean meat was never a problem but I've had trouble avoiding the other two as you'll see a bit further on.

I've never witnessed the ceremony so I can't say for certain what it entailed but if I had to guess—based on my observations of other priestly devotions—I would wager that there were a lot of sober facial expressions appropriate to the gravity of the situation plus some reading out from the scrolls and much heavy talk. Maybe my father had to answer a few questions saying *So I do* or *Yes I shall*. The ceremony was rounded out perhaps with a bit of incense and a few sips of the holy wine I had just been forever barred from tasting.

And that was it: the path of my life was laid out true and straight for all my days.

Manue my father kept close watch as I grew. Hovering over me like some bird of prey ensuring that I understood the expectation that had been placed like a cloak upon me. He spent much time making clear the difference between my people the Israelites and the other wretched bands of unfortunates occupying this land.

—Two things set us apart, he was fond of saying.—God is one. The law is the other.

At four years of age I stared up at him and nodded wordlessly.

—God and the law he said.—Both are sacred and both must be followed or else all collapses into anarchy and pointlessness.

At six years of age I gazed into his eyes and mulled his words.

—Without the law he said often and with satisfaction—we are no better than brutes or dogs. Or Philistines. Do you understand? Men require rules. We've got them.

At eight years of age I looked down upon my father's face and murmured agreement.

He went on—But it is Yahweh who truly sets us apart. It is His law we follow and not our own. It can seem harsh but so is the age we live in.

I thought on these words and they made sense to me so I took them to heart. There they seemed to reside within me and take root and grow even as I did.

Later he would tell me specifically—These are capital crimes: Murder. Killing another man's livestock or wife or children. Willful arson against another man's home or crops. Adultery. Or falsely accusing another man of any of these things so as to bring ruin upon him.

Most of this I could follow but one thing confused me.— What's adultery?

My father stared at me with a heaviness in his jowls.—I'll tell you later.

By the time I was eight years old I was half a head taller than my father and twice as powerful as any man. I could yoke a team of buffalo and drive them to the far horizon at a trot and if they collapsed before sundown I could hitch the plow around my shoulders and jog back home breaking new furrows as I went. I feared neither oxen nor buffalo nor camel: all could be made docile by my hand and sent cantering with a swat against their flanks. And about this ability let me tell you something else. At times when faced with a stubborn intractable beast I conversed with it. I don't mean that I spoke words aloud—no more at least than any other man. Rather I cleared my mind in a way prompted by some other impulse and directed my thoughts towards the creature and often I received thoughts in return. And this happened not only with dumb animals but with all the voiceless cold clay of the LORD's creation. Fallen trees & deep-rooted stumps heavy boulders & so forth. Anything you may think of and many a heavy burden was made lighter by this means.

Doubtless you consider me raving or simple to which I say: Believe as you like. But I've had many occasions to draw on this talent and it has served me well.

Seasons wheeled past as they are wont to do. By my tenth birthday I was famous in the region and so were my deeds which grew more impressive with each retelling. My mother's sisters doted on me and I strove to make them and my father proud. Somehow I had become a topic of twilight conversation: the villagers exaggerated my actions while embroidering my past and prophesying great things for my future.

By now I had grown fully sensible of the expectation laid at my feet—that I was a champion for my people who must somehow drive the Philistines from our land. And my mind became preoccupied with thoughts of conflict and battle. I could ride a horse well enough but had little experience of arms. To Manue I asked—Should I not train with a sword?

His face clouded.—Why?

—If I am to become a great hero I should learn the best way to slaughter my enemies.

He winced at this.—Don't concern yourself overly much with such things. You'll manage.

—But how?

He reached up to place a hand on my shoulder.—Trust in the LORD my son. If He wants you to fight you will fight. If not you won't. If He chooses you as His champion well then— nothing will prevent you.

That made sense I supposed.—And when He wants me to kill I said—He will give strength to my arm whether I hold a sword or not. Or whether I use it as other men say I ought.

Manue my father nodded slowly. His lips made a little pucker-ing shape that they got sometimes when considering a proposition in business or elsewhere.—Something like that he said finally.

Still the villagers gossiped. I cared little enough for this but ad-mit to enjoying the look of fear in men's eyes when they marked my approach. In women's eyes too there was often fear but sometimes something else and I had a notion that in time I would enjoy this even more.

Of beard I had none as yet but my hair was a thick black mass that my mother combed daily and with love. She seemed inordinately fond of this task: myself I would have chopped it off if I could but of course could not. The reasons why not had been carefully impressed upon me and I took them to heart as I had no desire to live as a weakling.

Sala would speak to me as she combed.—You must remember never to reveal your secret to anyone. The secret of your hair.

—Why would I ever do that?

—Promise me you won't.

—All right. But why would I be foolish enough to give someone such power over me?

And a funny look would pass over her face: wistful and amused at the same time.—Things are not always so clear. There may be . . . temptations.

—What kind of temptation could make me do something as stupid as that?

Her strange look would linger as if there were words she both wanted to speak and to forever hide from me her only offspring.—Ask your father.

—Why can't you tell me?

—It is something for men to discuss among themselves. Give me your promise that till then you will hold your secret close.

To which I duly agreed. What choice does a child have when talking to his beloved mother?

So it was that I entered my eleventh year of life. My hair had never been cut nor had I ever touched an intoxicating drink. Life coursed through me like vibration through a bell. My sinews toughened and bones grew strong. It's no boast to say that many called me handsome to look upon. Many but not all.

There was one who hated me. A sickly slanting youth my age named Hestil. I say slanting because he always reminded me of those vines that grow in regions with little sun and must creep along the earth rather than grow straight and tall towards the heavens. I say also that he was my age but really we were as unlike as it is possible for two boys to be. As if by reaching my strength and stature ahead of time I had somehow robbed him of his own for he was a weakling of a creature puny-shouldered with a waist like a girl's and a frail whining voice. His father's land bordered our neighbor's so there was but one farm between us and living in the same village we came across each other—not often but often enough for him to decide he hated me without cause other than the fact that I was tall and broad and already getting looks from women the likes of which he would never know. Looks and women both I mean.

Things might've gone on in this vein but for one day when I was in the hills outside our village and I came across the following scene. Hestil lying on the earth pink-faced with his leg twisted beneath him and a scattering of split logs. Not far off an ass standing by chuffing and scratching the earth with its hind feet. Hestil's breath coming in short ragged little gusts and the animal by all appearances much calmer.

Though I'm fast becoming a blind man now I wasn't one then. And even a blind man would've understood the situation: the boy piling wood on the stubborn animal and receiving a kick for his trouble. Or perhaps Hestil riding the ass but lacking the strength to control it and so being thrown. In any case he was my neighbor and my father had taught me that neighbors in need are to be helped. So I stepped forward and hailed Hestil so as not to surprise him there in his squalling and said—You appear hurt.

The boy turned his pouting lip towards me and didn't seem to like what he saw.—Aren't you brilliant he said.

I thought of offering my hand to lift him but couldn't think what I would do after that. Carrying him back to the village seemed unappealing for both of us. Meanwhile the ass stood and watched and occasionally tore up a tuft of grass so I moved towards it. The ass wheezed as I approached and shifted its hind feet. I emptied my mind of all thought but the one directed towards the beast: *Come to me. The boy needs you.*

The animal's own thoughts filled my head: *The boy is a fool.*
Well yes. But he is hurt.
He deserves nothing less.

Please.

The ass wheezed again and made a burp-nickering sound but let me place a hand on its bridle and then followed me back to the clearing where Hestil lay scowling harder than ever at the two of us and no doubt storing up new items in his inventory of hate.

—Here I said and held out my arm.—Let me help you up.

—Go away he said.—That beast is evil.

It was like talking to the ass again. I said—Don't be foolish. You're hurt and we've got to get you home.

—Go away now or you'll be sorry he said. It was more of a sneer than actual talking. The kind of thing you hear from whiny children and I'm sure you've heard it yourself. He all but spat at me:—If you don't go now I shall make you wish you had.

At that age I was still unused to jeering and threats from men who were scared and weak. (That would come later.) Nor did I understand the danger they can pose so I did a stupid thing. I laughed at Hestil. I laughed and said—Just how will you do that?

—You'll see.

It was a puzzle indeed and I had little patience then as now for puzzles. A more straightforward man I've always been for better or worse: my appetites are clearly visible in me and not buried some distance beneath clever words or dissembling falsity or pointless threats. Why I'm fashioned this way and not some other I can't say except perhaps to think that my father's bluntness had some contributory effect on my own.

There was nothing to do but put the child on the ass against his wishes and lead the beast away which I duly did. Had I known what was to follow I would have left him there without another word but although the One True God has bestowed many talents upon me He has seen fit to withhold the gift of prophecy.

As I led the animal down the track between the hills my intent was to deliver child and beast to Hestil's farmstead: my own chore that morning was already forgotten so thoroughly that even now I can't recall why I was there in the first place.

By midday I had nearly left the hills behind when Hestil snatched the bridle from my hands and jabbed his knife into the flank of the ass. The blade was keen—for Hestil took pride in this—and the poor startled creature screeched a protest before spinning on its hind legs and cantering up the trail down which we had just come.

I stood mystified as they disappeared among the mulberry trees and scrappy hillside shrubs. There was a sunbird flitting through the feathery branches: shiny purple-black against the silvered green. In my confusion I stared at it for a time. I remember thinking how much more sense there was in many of God's creatures than in human beings. How much more logical and regular and predictable were the birds & insects beasts of the field & fish in the sea. That seemed to be the lesson I was meant to learn that particular day. And with that I dismissed Hestil's errant behavior and considered the episode over with.

How wrong I was.

The next morning at breakfast we heard the slow tread of footsteps outside our house. It was Hestil's father hailing my own from our yard and if I ever knew his name I've long forgotten it. My father invited him inside to eat with us but our visitor said—You'd best come outside for what I have to say will not sound well beneath your own roof.

My father stepped outside. Sala my mother and I watched

each other's eyes and I saw her brows arc upwards when Hestil's father said—And your son too as this concerns him.

I looked to the door and then at my mother once again and she shrugged as if to say—Go then.

Outside was yet early with the sun barely clearing the hills and shadows stretched long and flat across the dew. Early-morning haze hung in the air like the ghosts of the day before. Hestil's father was a gaunt hollowchested man but tall with knobby strong hands and a hawk's nose and the kind of pale eyes that can arrest someone from thirty yards away. I know this because that's what they did to me.

Behind me my mother leaned into the doorway. Manue my father said—Well then?

Hestil's father glared at us all and said—This child of yours—I shan't call him a boy—broke my son's leg and stole our ass.

This statement so astonished my father that he was left dumb. It was Sala my mother who said—When and where was this?

—Yesterday said our neighbor and pointed.—In the hills. He ambushed Hestil knocked him down and broke his leg. Then stole our donkey and drove him into the ravine.

My father found his voice.—Well fuck me brother. Was it injured?

—The animal is dead. My son's a cripple. Hestil's father's voice cracked and trembled as he spoke. Either he really believed the lies he was spouting or he could mimic better than anyone I had ever seen.—Hestil he said—was left to crawl on hands and one good knee for the entire afternoon before he was picked up by a caravan. God only knows what he's been through. The boy can hardly speak—

He broke off then as he could hardly speak himself. He wasn't lying that much was clear. Hestil of course was and I wondered what to do about it.

My mother slapped the back of my head.—Hey! I'm talking to you.

—Sorry I mumbled.—I was thinking.

—Do it later. You hear what this man says?

—Yes.

—Did you do those things?

—No.

My father exhaled softly. Hestil's father straightened up tall and stiff and said—You're calling me a liar?

—No sir. But your son hates me and he's saying things that aren't true.

He sneered the same way his child had and said—So none of this happened then. It's all just the boy's invention.

Quickly I described the day before. How I had come across Hestil and tried to help only to have him run off. When I came to the end though I knew my story had a flaw. Hestil's father pounced on it.

—What you're saying makes no sense.

Well there was no arguing that so I didn't bother.

—You're saying my son was getting rescued by you but instead decided to run off send his animal to die and then crawl back in agony on a broken limb to leave himself crippled for life. That's what you're saying.

—That's how it looks to me I said.

The old man scratched the gray fuzz edging his jaw.—And why exactly would he do that?

This of course was what I didn't know. But a glimmer of an idea had begun to shine in my mind as we spoke. I didn't know whether I should say anything but then decided there wasn't much else to do. So I said:—Stealing and killing livestock is a crime sir. Punishable by death.

Behind me my mother inhaled sharply. Manue shot me a look.

The jaw rubbing stopped.—You accuse my son of slandering you so that you're executed? That's not how I raise my children.

My father looked ready to break something. He cleared his throat and it sounded like stones would come out. He said— And I never taught my son to cripple weaklings and steal the neighbor's livestock. So one of us at least did a pisspoor job of raising his child.

Hestil's father hurled at Manue such a dirty look as you've never seen but if he said anything to this I don't remember what it was.

The Tribunal

The men of Dan set a day for the tribunal. If there had been a judge in the land at the time he would've been asked to preside but we had none so it was to be decided through debate and consensus. This could take some time especially as my case had grown famous in the region as swiftly as if locusts carried the news. Both Hestil and I were alleging capital crimes one against the other—he accusing me of slaughtering livestock and me accusing him of false witness—and though we were both but boys these allegations were taken seriously. If the tribunal decided against me it would be rough going and not unthinkable that they would invoke the ultimate penalty given my size and strength and alleged misdeeds.

—What will happen? I asked my father more than once but he merely looked away.

My mother was more helpful.—Your birth was prophesied by an angel of the LORD she said.—He has a special destiny for you and will allow no harm to come of this.

This was heartening but not entirely convincing. It is the rare mother in this world who would say—With a little bad luck you'll probably die. So it was with no lack of foreboding that I waited for the day of judgment to arrive. Really it felt like I was waiting for that other Day of Judgment that will come to every man and woman but with this difference: I knew its precise date which is not true for the other. Even my appetite disappeared for the first time that I could remember (and the last). Though it was only a period of three days it felt much longer.

When the morning finally came my father accompanied me to the little clearing in the village center behind the granary where the men and elders sat in a circle upon cubes of sandstone worn smooth by generations of backsides. The neighboring villagers not directly affected but curious nonetheless squatted in the dirt behind them and the young boys stood some ways off. Altogether there were close to a hundred people in that small space. The women of course were not present and wouldn't be allowed to witness the proceedings or otherwise interfere.

Hestil and I squatted on the ground facing the men who would decide our fate. There was no judge as I said nor any particular authority but there were plenty of elderly men and after a time some of them said—Let's get on with it or words to that effect. One grandfather in particular seemed keen. I knew him by sight and reputation: his beard was mainly dark but with thick strands of white running down like ropes from the corners of his mouth and he was famous for his squawking voice and foul temper.

He directed Hestil to stand in the middle of the circle and tell his story which was familiar to me but I was shocked at his appearance. His skin had gone sallow and his leg dragged useless behind him: calling him a cripple had been no exaggeration by his father. He leaned upon a stick to remain upright and at that he looked none too steady. Despite myself I felt a little sorry for him as it's no joke being a crippled farmer and his usefulness in the field was clearly ended and he would be a charity case from that time forward. A burden unto his family—worse even than a daughter—and unlikely ever to marry or sire children of his own. Even if he did he would merely be a burden unto them too. At the same time it was difficult to maintain sympathy for someone who was trying so hard to buy his broken future with the coin of my own life.

While I was still thinking this Hestil's tale ended and I was bid to stand and tell my side of the story which I did and then sat down.

Murmurings and mutterings and heavy sighs ran thick among the men. I gathered from the scowls and other looks of impatience that they were dissatisfied with the stalemate as it was just Hestil's word and my own contradicting each the other and no end to it in sight. Hestil was told to stand and answer a great many questions which he did and then I was told to do the same. Presumably they were looking for inconsistencies in our stories but could find none either in my own telling or Hestil's.

Some of the men carried scrolls in their laps containing I suppose the laws of my people. The writing on these scrolls was—and still is—as meaningful to me as so many animal droppings but these men made a great show of agonizing over them as if expecting enlightenment from the LORD Himself. It seemed they got none though for no matter how hard they squinted at the marks and whispered urgently back and forth they never found any advice on how to make Hestil's story lie compliantly alongside mine. I admit I would have been mightily surprised if they had. So they went back to questioning us again. It was by now early afternoon and I was growing parched and tired but it seemed a poor time to mention this. Anyway Hestil looked worse.

They asked Hestil yet again:—Describe how Samson killed your ass. And he said:—He lifted it and hurled it over the cliff into the ravine. It was still struggling even in his arms but he carried it easily as only he could do.

One of the village men agreed—That's where we found it and another said—Then we brought it back to the farm. And all the men looked at me and saw that I could easily do this thing and they were afraid. At that moment I was not so well pleased as before to mark the fear on their faces.

The old man with the creaky voice and ropey white in his beard said to me—Yet you claim Hestil ran off on the ass.

—Yes.

—What exactly did he do?

I thought about it. It was only a few days earlier but seemed much longer. I said—He pulled the bridle from me and rode back up the trail into the hills. I wasn't expecting such and anyway my eyes were on the trail which was uneven and rough.

—And that was all? the village men pressed.—He took the bridle and the ass bolted?

I knew this was important and tried hard to remember.—

Not exactly I said.—He . . . hit it. Hit the animal's rump. And as I said this I remembered exactly. I said—He jabbed its flank with the knife and it spun around and cantered up the path. Yes. That was the last I saw of them.

I looked over at Hestil and saw now his fear but didn't realize what I had just said. He understood something that still eluded me.

The old man called to him—Is this what happened?

—No! Hestil stammered.—I didn't—I mean *he* jabbed the ass with a knife—

The old man's frown was fierce.—You didn't say so before. Why would he do such a thing?

Hestil could barely speak for stuttering:—To make it jump off the cliff—

All the men and boys shifted and swayed as if a wind blew through them. Several called out together—You said he lifted it in his arms—You said he threw it—*You* said—

—Yes well no. Not exactly. Let me speak!

—Picked it up as only he could do the men kept saying.—Threw it over still struggling that's what you said.

I was beginning to understand and hope flickered in me like a candle in a storm.

Hestil's voice was tiny.—He did. He *did.*

The elder with twin ropes of white in his beard looked in a foul temper—as if if Hestil had been his own grandson he would've given him a thrashing then and there. Well I couldn't blame him. He said—So if you're telling the truth the animal should be unmarked. And if *he's* telling the truth there should be a wound.

He glared at me.—Isn't that right?

—I don't know I said.—He only sort of jabbed it. Slapped it

really—it's not like he stabbed it so I don't know how much of a hole there'd be. But if there is one it'll be on the left flank for that's the hand that held the knife. Everyone knows Hestil favors his left hand.

—That's right nodded some of the villagers. The old man's mouth was set in a downward arc.—Let's look at least.

Hestil's wide-open eyes reflected no light.

So they looked and what should they find but a shallow nick on the left flank just where I said it'd be. Hestil had often bragged to the other boys about the keen edge he kept on his knives but now I bet he wished he'd been a little less attentive. I've noticed that the weak man often takes undue pride in possessing powerful weapons but in this case at least it proved his undoing.

We waited in the village while perhaps a dozen men went and looked at the animal before returning to tell us what they'd found. Three of the dozen weren't convinced it was a knife wound but admitted it could be. The others thought it probably was. Hestil started trembling so roughly I feared he would break his other leg. I said before he'd always been weak and now he was crippled and afraid to die besides. The sight of him sickened me.

He kept saying—It got hurt when he threw it. It got cut on a rock when it landed on the ground.

Mainly the men ignored him but one said—The wound is too clean for a stone to have made. There's a clear puncture in the flesh like this—And he held up his fingers in a V to indicate a cut made by a knife point.

—It's an old wound Hestil moaned.—It happened a few days ago when I was frustrated. I forgot to mention it to the tribunal. Don't kill me. I don't want to die.

But no one was listening. Even his own father had joined the men huddled over the scrolls. There was some kind of argument going on about the law and with a hundred different opinions you can imagine how long it lasted and how much anybody was actually listening to anyone else. Only a handful could read the scrolls but that didn't stop everyone from having a strong opinion nor was shyness a common quality among the men in my village. So the horde of them gabbled on like a family of crows. It was only after the sun had hobbled all the way across the sky like a beggar looking for someplace to rest that the voices dropped off little by little. Even then the ones that were left weren't necessarily the ones who were right but they had the stamina to keep talking longer than anyone else. Such is often the way an issue gets resolved.

What they decided was this. I was innocent and Hestil was guilty of slandering me which was a capital crime since he had accused me of a capital crime. But he was still a child and unmarried and in his parents' care so the village was reluctant to stone him. And since I was a child as well they would grant me the right to pardon him. If I so wished. This they explained to me with great care and asked if I understood and I said—Yes. Then they asked would I pardon him and I looked at his pathetic bleating face and twisted leg and stunted frame and hollowchested father and I remembered the many lectures from my own father Manue and I said:—No.

And the men shifted and scuffed the earth with their sandals and looked down and mumbled—Well that's your right after all. But the old man with the white ropes in his beard said— It's been a long day for all of us—why don't you think on it tonight and we can reconvene tomorrow.

—There's no need for that I said and I meant it. He

would've killed me in his place and been glad of it. The law made no allowance for mercy and I saw no need for it either so I said—Let's not waste any more time.

—Well now said one of the men.

I hefted the nearest slab of sandstone. Three or four normal men would've struggled together to lift it but I raised it one-armed over my head and said—The law is the basis for everything we believe. It *is* what we *are*. If you'll not discharge your duty I will.

My father had taught me well and I knew I was right.

An awkward silence then as the men looked anywhere but at me or at Hestil who lay openmouthed on the ground making no sound as he cried in a helpless silent way. As if the stones had already broken his flesh. I couldn't stand it. With a swift movement I hurled the rock and broke his head apart and slew him quicker than he deserved. The sandstone being soft splintered apart as well so there was a thick slurry of blood & brains dust & red stone chips smeared on the ground. A little moan escaped Hestil's father and some of the other men flinched but I knew enough of the law to know that as the accused I had the right to throw the first stone.

And as it turned out the last. To their credit some of the other men had rocks in their hands but when they saw the crimson smear of Hestil's head draining into the sand they let them drop.

The business was done and the women would be called to clean up. I turned for home with my father behind me speaking not a word and me feeling a tremendous sense of relief. As we approached the farm my mother ran into the fields to take me in her arms and squeeze my shoulders and—the only time

I remember her doing this—cry quietly. She clung to me as we walked back to the house while her sisters clucked around her like hens for they had left their own homes to keep vigil with her. Inside the house Sala fussed over me and fed me fine cuts of lamb my favorite meat. She watched closely while I ate and I ate a lot. I was famished and exhausted after my ordeal and who could blame me? After supper I rose to go to sleep.

—You seem different my mother said before I went to my quarter.—Something has changed in you since this morning.

—I'm just tired I said.

And Manue my father said—He's different all right. He won't ever be the same again. And there was some quality in Manue's voice that made Sala turn towards him with a worried look and left me feeling uncomfortable—as if the day's judgment wasn't yet done. But I was too weary for all this. I bid them goodnight and lay down on my pallet and was asleep in an instant. I slept through the night like the free man I was with no disturbing dreams uncertainties or shades of gray to interfere with the comforting surety of black and white.

The law had been upheld & the guilty punished the innocent defended & order maintained. Truly I had begun to understand what it meant to be a champion of the LORD.

The next morning I woke refreshed as if life held countless possibilities as yet hidden and undisclosed. The sun was shining outside. I smiled and remembered my mother's words from days earlier. She had been speaking about the One True God Himself when she said:

—He has a special destiny for you.

The Priest Again

Every day my vision grows worse. I was half-blind when I got here and now can make out only the murky outlines of things floating around me like spectres while the firelight glows orange in the center of everything as if the sun itself has descended to witness my humiliation.

This morning—for so I think it was but time has no real meaning in this place of perpetual carousal and if my ears don't deceive me orgiastic iniquity—the Philistine priest Meth or Menth approached yet again to mock me saying—Soon now it shan't be long.

Wishing to show myself unflustered I said—Soon what?

He chuffed like a barnyard animal and rubbed his hands. Or so I guessed as my nervous imagination pictured what my poor shadowy vision could not.—Soon he said—justice shall be served and the dead shall enjoy their vengeance.

—How is that exactly? I asked.—Do the Philistines plan to throw themselves into the sea?

He leaned close.—We shall cut out your heart and roast it and pass it round on a platter for all to enjoy their fill. And while so eating we shall close our eyes and call to mind our beloved dead who lie murdered at your hands and those of your fellows.

This was not the first time I've played host to threats such as these so I said—I hope you're hungry because my heart is bigger than any man's.

But really this was bluff on my part. Tired I was this morning and the more so now and I've little doubt that a sharp knife and a strong arm would be adequate to do all he said and more.

—Hungry? the priest said.—Oh we are hungry enough that's certain. No need to worry on that account. After all we have had ahh years to work up our appetite. Decades in fact of suffering beneath the heel of your arbitrary violence. Wouldn't you agree?

There was no point answering so I only stood there wondering how many days I had left to live and this was no happy moment believe me. For that matter I knew not how long I had been imprisoned already as I constantly slip in and out of alertness and my mind wanders even when awake. As you well know. Certainly I've been in confinement for weeks now though I've been chained to these pillars in this hall only for some few days: before this I was for the most part confined to a stinking underground cell. I'm filthy and unwashed and my legs cramp balefully and my scalp is aflame with itching and rash. Even though my hair is shorn my scalp cries out in agony as if trying to grow it back day by day and—sometimes I feel sure of this—it is succeeding.

The priest slunk off soon thereafter leaving me again to reflect bitterly on my confinement and the events that led to it. The most obvious being my miscalculations regarding a certain woman. But if I'm to tell this story as it happened I suppose I must tell it in its entirety and that means all the women in my life not merely the last.

Now you had best prepare yourself for henceforth comes the sinning & violence lust & murder you've been awaiting so eagerly.

Women

I should tell you a few things about women. If you're the type to get easily scandalized then perhaps you should skip to the next part which is about marriage and might suit your tastes better. (Though I warn you my marriage turned out to be none too orthodox either.) But I've always been a plainspoken individual and see no reason to change this now.

Maybe this comes from my father Manue. I remember once when I was a youth him laying his hand on my shoulder and saying—Son do this for me. Endeavor to make every sentence you speak worthy to serve as your last. You never know when death will come for you and your last words are what people will remember you by. Imagine the shame of dying suddenly and having your final words be some petty falsehood.

At the time I thought this was fine advice and I still think so. It wasn't till much later that it occurred to me to wonder whether Manue's favorite expressions such as—Fuck me brother! would have fit his ideal as worthy last words. But by then I had left my home far behind and was unable to ask him.

I forget now what had occasioned his remarks. Most likely some unpleasant encounter with a dishonest caravan or crooked merchant—for there was never any shortage of these and from what I saw they were equally well supplied by all the tribes.

So then. All I mean to say as I stand here in chains in what is probably the final portion of my life is this: Honesty seems an even more precious commodity than ever before.

Let me tell you then about women.

The truth is that I liked women and most of them liked me. All of them had an opinion about me and for many this opinion was favorable. At fifteen I was a head taller than most grown men and by sixteen I had filled out that lanky frame with sinew and bulk. Some women will tell you that they care nothing for the looks of a man seeing only what's in his heart as important and to that I say: Save it for someone else. From my own experience I know there are few women alive who will choose to look upon—or lie with—an ugly man if there's a comely one nearby.

Men as we all know are just the same but they lie about it less.

Now the fact was that many women were made uncomfortable to look upon a man of my size and so kept their distance. Doubtless there were some who felt nothing more complex than simple fear. But others were willing to seek time in my presence and some few were even prepared to risk much by acting on their basest impulses.

By this time I understood what adultery was. Like theft it is a capital crime and not a thing to be undertaken lightly. Yet with this as with many things the appearance of a situation is often more important than the reality of it. Not always but often. And from my experiences with the other tribes of Canaan I would hazard to guess that it is so for most people. Sometimes it strikes me that controlling the urge to mate has been the guiding principle of all human society since Adam and Eve stepped forth from their paradise that first morning. And like them most of us have failed in our attempts at control.

By now you shouldn't be surprised at my meanderings. I was talking about women.

The first who had me was a widow of more than forty sum-

mers who came upon me while I was bathing in the river some
distance away from our village. Dusk was falling and I had
been laboring all day and was sore and filthy from coping with
a team of uncommonly stubborn oxen. So I did not bathe in
my customary manner which is to say quickly. Instead I lingered in the shallow pool—floating with my legs apart and my
arms outstretched—gazing at the sky overhead as it passed
through turquoise to bruise-purple. At length I stood and
turned towards the bank where my clothes were and surprised
I was to see this woman squatting there.

—Hello I said covering my loins.

She nodded and stared quite openly at me which is considered ill manners but in later years I forgave her this rudeness
as she was many years a widow and both her young sons had
died the winter before: everyone said these calamities changed
her. Probably she hadn't seen a grown man's naked body for
quite some time. So I made my way towards the bank giving
up any attempt at covering myself saying only: My clothes are
with you.

Instead of answering she shrugged and her robe slipped off
and suddenly she was naked on the ground before me and
open. I responded as any sixteen-year-old would respond and
went in her.

—Oh she said. As if she were about to say more but then
didn't.

Her thighs clamped around me and I rubbed against them
too and her belly rose up against my loins as I went in.

A few moments later I was done and I got off her and stood
up. She lay there watching me. She was not especially pretty or
shapely although a life of labor in the fields had kept her flesh
somewhat sinewy. Mostly white her hair shined up from the

brown earth and leaf mold. But the best parts of her body were her ankles which were slender and firm as if carved from dark wood and polished smooth. To this day I have a weakness for ankles. Her worst feature was her mouth: even as she lay there it looked at me pinched and curled like a caterpillar that had been hit. I asked—Did you like that? hoping to uncurl that caterpillar at least a little but all she said was—It'll do.

I looked around. Night was collecting so I said—I have to get home.

—Already? she said.—I just got here. She lolled a little and her bosoms pointed away to the woods on each side and I liked that. When she opened herself I saw my seed spilling out of her like a string of white beads and I liked that even more. So I knelt down between her again and went in.

—Oh—Oh—*Oh*—that *hurts*—

It wasn't hurting me.

—Careful—

The second time took longer but felt better when it finished. The sun was well down then and when I said—I have to go she didn't argue or say—So soon?

—Can we do this again tomorrow?

She took some time to answer.—I don't know.

—Why not?

—Let me think about it she said.

She was pulling on her clothes but I was already dressed so I turned away.—Don't think too long I said.—I will be here this time tomorrow if you want.

Then I felt like I was being abrupt so I stopped and looked back.—I never did that before I said.—It was nice. Thank you.

She didn't say anything but maybe she nodded and I couldn't see it. Anyway the next day at dusk I went to the same spot but she didn't come nor the evening after that. I got the message and stopped waiting for her. After that we would see each other from time to time in the village or at festivals or weddings and even though I sometimes caught her looking at me she never said anything besides—Hello Samson when I nodded to her. So I guess she had gotten what she wanted. And what that was exactly I'm not sure. A few years later I heard she fell ill on some spoiled grain that left her retching out her innards for three nights and then she died.

Some Others

That woman wasn't the only one of course. There were others—never a lot all at once like some men brag about but a steady trickle. For a time it seemed I was never more than a few months away from having lain with a woman.

Mainly these were strangers. I learned quickly that local women were interested too but after a bad experience with a husband from the next village over I decided I should avoid coveting my neighbor's wife so to speak. So then I limited my exploring to women I met while away from home. This became easier as I began traveling farther afield to assist in my father's business.

The other thing I learned was to avoid virgins. For the most part this was no trouble since virgins as a rule avoided me. Married women were better able to accommodate me and the more so if they'd had children. Virgins were troublesome with their expectations and tears and I swore them off completely after a particularly bloody incident with a slim-hipped Canaanite girl who surprised me on the trail down from the mountains. Olive-eyed and willowy she was a change from the matrons who usually welcomed me but I thought *Why not?* and grew happier still when I disrobed her and beheld her smooth body and firm flanks and flaring backside. Fair she was as if the daughter of a wealthy man and not some girl used to hard work and I grew even more sure of this when I found her feet soft and uncalloused. You may believe me when I say few girls went about with soft soles in those days. Or these days either for that matter. Her fingertips were soft too and I put them in my mouth and she giggled and for a moment I swore she was no more than fourteen years old.

On impulse I asked—Does you father know you're here?

She giggled again and said—Are you mad?

Then she trailed her fingers through my beard and said—It's so soft it's like feathers.

This was because my mother Sala combed out my hair and beard every evening after supper. She sat on a stool behind me and ran a wooden comb through the strands as the light outside faded from dusk to blackness. Her touch was gentle as only a mother's can be and well did I enjoy these nightly sessions though as a young boy they had left me fidgety and impatient. Then however thinking of Sala felt strange as I stood looking upon this girl and wanting to go in her. So I put aside thoughts of my mother and reached for this girl's hips and said—Let's get away from this trail.

But all our light feeling and happiness soured when she lay flat and unable to restrain myself I pushed my way in and she started cringing and whining and protesting. She made so much noise I felt sure someone would hear so I had to cover her mouth while I finished. Which fortunately I did in a short time for she thrashed about in a most exciting way. When I was done I got a good look for the first time and can honestly say I was appalled at the blood staining her thighs and mine. I knew I was big but she must've been uncommonly small and this was my first inkling that some unions are simply doomed from the start.

—Are you all right? I asked. It's no shame to admit I felt scared. I had lain with several women by this time but had left none bloodied and weeping in the dirt.

She didn't answer—just lay there crying quietly with her face covered in tears and snot.

What became of her I never learned. Maybe nothing in particular. I dressed quickly and left her there to collect herself. The incident left a bad feeling and from then on I foreswore virgins: I would limit myself to big-hipped harlots and matrons and widows. Such women took me as I was and didn't change their minds halfway through or cry out in pain. This was a vow I managed to keep with only one exception which was when I decided to marry. And that turned out to be yet another incident with dire consequences—as you shall see.

Huneisha

My eighteenth year had come and gone when I traveled to the Philistine village called Thamnatha which was some days' travel west from my home. My father had acquired a quantity of ceramic pottery vessels which he desired to trade for incense and spices from the Edomites who regularly brought such products from the deserts to the east and south. My people had little enough intercourse with the Edomites who did some business with the Philistines but it was thought worthwhile that I try my hand there. I suppose there was the thought also that my size and bulk might protect me should any Philistine take it into his head to do me mischief on the road. So I brought a pair of companions with me—strong men both and skilled with the sword but only two so we wouldn't be mistaken for a raiding party—and loaded the asses and went on our way.

Before leaving I asked Manue something which had puzzled me for a time.—Father does our law apply to the Edomites and Philistines or only to ourselves?

To which he looked confused and rubbed the bridge of his nose.—I'm not sure I follow you son.

I sought to explain.—Must I treat with these other tribes as I would with our own people? Or since they fail to observe the law themselves is it acceptable that I disregard it as well?

Manue looked as though something unpleasant rested in his mouth.—It would be unwise to cheat any man he said.—Word might spread and then you would have a fight on your hands with him and all his kin as well. That's not something that would benefit anyone.

I thought on this and found it sensible but still it didn't exactly answer my question.—But just suppose I said.—Suppose some Philistine committed a grave insult against me and I took his life in recompense. In passion let's say. Would our law—Israelite law—hold me guilty?

At this Manue looked troubled indeed.—Perhaps I should accompany you to Thamnatha.

—No Father. Nothing will happen. I'm just curious.

This failed to lighten his mood any that I could see. But at length he answered—No Israelite tribunal would execute you for such a crime against another tribe. Of course the others will have some manner of justice themselves to which you might I suppose be accountable. If they could catch you of course.

—And adultery? I said. For I was old enough now to understand the word as well as to consider my actions with the neighboring women including the young girl of whom I've already spoken. I had no desire to be stoned to death for the sake of some Canaanite.

Manue's expression grew if anything even gloomier. He leaned towards me so that his eyes peered out from under his heavy brows.—The same is true for any crime that we recognize. We follow Yahweh's law to give order to our own existence but other tribes who choose to spurn His word must also live without His protection.

This made sense to me and I said so. But Manue my father looked troubled nonetheless and watched closely after me as I left with my companions.

At Thamnatha we discovered that the Edomite caravan had passed through days before. The local men squinted at us with no great love but none gave trouble and when we turned to go my eye fell upon a girl slouching in the doorway of a hut turning wool on a spindle. I admit I stared for her face was long and narrow like a fox's and as her fingers played over the fibers I wondered what it would feel like to have them play over me. She must've noticed me too for she looked up with her eyes like wells and said—What? in a mischievous way.

I wasn't thirsty but I said—Have you some water for a tired traveler?

She brought it and stood there and was tiny. She watched my hands as I drank as if to make sure I didn't break the jug. I was shaking so much I might have. I was by this time at my full height and broad besides and could've easily fit two of her slender frames inside my own or maybe three. Still she stared up at me with a smile as if she understood something I didn't and my head was full of pictures of her flat on the ground with me on her going in.

The incident of the bloody virgin was nagging at the back of my memory but somehow this girl seemed different. That one had been delicate and fine and unused to rough handling—but this one gave the impression of having a resilience and scrappiness that could withstand even me. Whether this was true or simply the result of my overheated imagination I can't say. But she certainly seemed like a girl who wouldn't start weeping at every little thing. She seemed more like the type who would lash out at that which discomfited her like some feisty little woodland creature.

Probably you're thinking that this is an awful lot to conclude just from seeing a girl in a doorway and drinking her water. To which I can only say: Maybe you're right but I was there and you weren't.

I asked her—What's your name?

—Huneisha she said.

I said—Are you married? and she said—Not yet.

I looked around. I needed to distract myself from the smell coming off her like oil. In fact it probably was olive oil in her hair that made it so shiny like the purple-black feathers of a sunbird but I was still a youth then and although I had lain with women I was yet unschooled in the wiles that girls are taught and have perfected since the time of Eve to snare their prey and keep it within easy reach. My traveling companions were some ways off with our animals eager to depart so as to avoid camping more than two nights on the way home. The other villagers kept their distance too though many sly looks passed our way. Handing the jug back to her I said very softly—Do you want to be?

She blinked. The lashes that came down and swept back up were like butterfly wings.—Want to be what? she asked.

—Married.

At that she blushed and I knew I had her. Breathing in my chest grew even larger and I shuffled a half step closer and she didn't move away.—My father will contact yours I said.

She said nothing only gazed at her feet and bit her lip. I knew then that I would want her forever.

I admit to acting impulsively but there was more to it than just my loins pointing the way. At certain moments in life we feel a powerful pull to someone we have just met. It can strike unexpectedly but is no less strong for that—in fact this very suddenness makes it even more powerful. I've heard warriors speak of this feeling among their comrades: one moment is enough to know *I will risk my life for this person* and I have my-self felt something of this intensity in certain meetings with women. Perhaps you have never experienced it for yourself in which case I can say only: I feel sorry for you.

For the three days' journey back I didn't sleep I just stared at the nighttime sky and repeated her name. Huneisha. And sometimes I felt myself and imagined that she was touching me or I her. Thinking of her drove all the other women from my imagination and they receded in my memory. In the morn-ings on the trail the lack of sleep hampered me not at all. In fact I so hounded and pressed my companions that at length they begged me to leave them and go on ahead at my own pace which I duly did.

Manue my father was not well pleased to see me return from Thamnatha with neither incense nor spices pottery nor even my companions or our animals. He grew even less pleased when I said—Father I've seen the girl I wish to marry. She is a Philistine named Huneisha in the village of Thamnatha and she is unmarried and willing. I beg you Father accept her as wife for me.

And I fell to my knee as I said this so he would mark my seriousness.

We were standing in the courtyard between the house and his workshop. He had been digging out a grain silo and now stood waist-deep in a brick-lined hole so even though I was on my knee he still had to look up at me when he said:—Eh?

I explained it all again. He called for Sala my mother and with her came her youngest sister Norum who had never married. And when they joined us I was left to explain yet a third time. I had expected them to be glad—my wanderings with other men's wives were not entirely secret and I had thought they would welcome this sign of my settling down. But it was not to be.

Sala was no more pleased than my father.—Is there no girl among our own people that would suit you? Must it be this Philistine? I'm sure we can find someone better.

Though it pained me to contradict her I spoke up and said—There is none better and no other I want.

Awkwardness settled around us for a time.—Such unions can be difficult said my father.

So they could but I had little care for that. I told you before how sometimes the Philistines were in the ascendant and sometimes one tribe or another of Canaanites and at other times the desert tribes like the Edomites or else my own people. It was an uncertain changeable back-and-forth but it concerned mainly the residents of towns and cities and those living along the trade routes. For villagers like us there was less concern. Of course sometimes there would be a calling to the villages and a huge army would gather for a battle or a siege and then it was everyone's business for the outcome of the battle could determine the fortunes of the whole land for a generation or more. Such stories as that of Debbora show this well. But no such epic had occurred since the days of Gedeon who defeated the Madianites with just three hundred men and then Jephte who with his army slew forty-two thousand Ephraimites who had refused to fight the Ammonites but who later claimed to be angry for missing out. At this time in our history a sort of uneasy balance prevailed among the different peoples and intermarriage—like trade—was not unheard of.

So I said to my reluctant parents—Come and see her and you'll understand.

But my father's frown was colossal.—It will not go well he said.—They are not even circumcised.

This confused me to the point that I was speechless for a little while. It was difficult to see why circumcision should play such a decisive part in my choice of a bride. I said—Father I want to marry the girl not her brothers. She pleases me to look on and speak to. (And to smell but I knew not to say that.)—Please at least come and see her.

To this my mother's sister Norum murmured—No harm in that is there? and for this I felt grateful to her.

At length my parents consented though grudgingly.

So we went some days later to Thamnatha and approached from the east: myself Manue and Sala. At this time the villages of the Philistines were larger than ours and occupied better land—the broad fertile plain between the western ocean and the ridge of mountains that ran down the center of Canaan like a backbone and from which my people wrenched their existence. I don't complain: such a life makes us tough and in any case it's what the LORD desires for us. But the Philistine plains were fertile and easy to plow and thick with olive groves and vineyards and I would be dishonest to say it never crossed my mind—while passing through them—how settling in such a place would make a man feel he had a chance at a long peaceful life and a fruitful one.

So it was something of a shock when the lion attacked us.

It will be remembered that Canaan was a wilder place some years back than it is now and even now it can be rather rough-edged. Lions and other beasts though rare were not unheard of. This lion was a small male barely grown that had probably wandered north in search of a territory of its own. Well I couldn't blame it but neither could I abide its growling and roaring and fetid moldering-meat breath and my parents frozen in shock between the waist-high rows of grapevines glowing with the rich goldengreen of the lowering sun. My mother spoke not a peep while my father grumbled oaths and passed his sword from hand to hand. That weapon looked like a child's toy and the lion was no child. It will be remembered too that they were neither of them terribly young.

Fortunately for them I was. Moreover something came over me then and I would call it a trance or calmness or some such supernatural state but really I know it was the breath of the LORD gusting through me and even as the lion hurled itself forward so too did I leap upon it and grasp its jaws and force its head back and push and push as it butted its brow against my chest so I grappled all the harder to wrench its head and I felt the sinews fight and tighten and resist and for a long few moments it could have gone either in my favor or the beast's but then all at once the bones gave way and the snapping of its neck ran up my biceps like a trail of ants while its body spasmed and claws tremored against the air and thrashed as I twisted and rents appeared in its flesh and crimson froth bubbled from its jaws in a thick foam that sprayed across me and stung meaty and metallic in my eyes and lungs as I twisted the head round and round and opened the jaws wide wide wider than they were meant to go and the jaw tore away in my hand the head tore away the limbs thrashed one final time though the life was already spent and the whole body collapsed limp into the dust between the vines and then I got on with the business of tearing apart the beast one piece from the next as the power of the LORD coursed through me like Life itself or maybe Death.

Some time later I looked up. There was no lion anymore there were just sticky pieces of things in the dirt. The sun was setting by now and its red light splashed across the nearby vines as if wet.

My parents huddled some distance away my father ashen-faced and my mother weeping. Truly the lion had frightened them.

To comfort them I held out a handful of sinews and said—See? It can't hurt you now.

My father swallowed and nodded but Sala my mother was so upset she just clung to his side. I thought then of telling them of the frenzy of God that had filled me during the fight but decided they had had enough of supernatural concerns for one day. Instead I said to them—It's done here. Shall we go?

—Yes indeed said my father standing up. He pulled Sala to

her feet and gave me a searching look that I couldn't interpret. But I was filled with light when he said—Let's go find this Philistine girl my son. Let's get you married as quick as we can.

The Preparations

If only I had known what was to come I wouldn't have been so keen. How many men were to die—and women too—on account of this wedding? But of course I knew none of this and pressed forward like a wolf with my nose to the trail. I thought Huneisha would become my wife and give me sons but instead she would be dead by winter: murdered by a mob of her own people.

Truly it's good we can't see the future for it would so fill us with despair that we would do no other than sit howling in the night. But in this as in every other particular the One True God has revealed His infinite wisdom and mercy.

Our fathers met and made arrangements. What Manue and Sala thought of Huneisha they didn't say but nor did they raise any objection so make of that what you will. Huneisha's family received my parents with great courtesy and accepted them into their home until such time as the wedding would take place. This was to be in a few days. Gifts were exchanged between the families and more gifts paid to the bride—some from my parents and some from her own. Huneisha was well pleased with all this as brides usually are. She seemed disappointed only with the ring I gave her to symbolize our union which was—in keeping with my people's custom—a simple loop of unadorned gold. Among the Philistines such a token was seen as niggardly in the extreme accustomed as they were to great bejeweled necklaces and silver bracelets that weigh heavy as armor and so forth.

To her credit Huneisha tried to conceal her disappointment but did a poor job of it. I was learning quickly that she was a girl who ever kept her feelings plain on her face and in this regard she was much like me.

—Is this all? she asked looking more confused than angry.

Sitting as we were with my parents and hers nearby and the smiles on all their faces growing more strained by the moment—though maybe for different reasons—I spoke quickly lest shame be brought upon my parents who had bestowed the ring upon me to give to her. I explained—It's our tradition. The circle has no beginning and no end. There is no stone to break its unity: it is complete as we shall be.

She bit her lip and nodded. I don't know whether she understood but she was trying to which was something I appreciated.

Fortunately there were many other gifts and dowries and so on—clothing & jewelry oils & perfume—that distracted my young wife-to-be from her disappointment.

There was also much feasting in honor of myself and my parents. And if you're astonished at such courtesy being extended from Philistines all I can say is that we were not actively at war and that even in times of war there are individual acts of civility among people. I should say also that my reputation was by now well established in the region not only amongst my own tribe and there are few people of any nation in the world who are unwilling to accept greatness into their midst. Perhaps this sounds immodest but I merely speak the truth. Great deeds came easily to me and more were soon to follow—though whether these deeds will be to your liking I can't say.

So then. I took advantage of these days to steal a chance encounter with Huneisha in the vineyard. It wasn't easy and all I could think to say when at last we were together was—Do you like the ring any better now?

She frowned again and looked at it on her hand.—It's growing on me she said.

I cast about for something else to say.—Soon we shall be wed.

—Yes. She smiled.

—And this pleases you?

—Why should it not? She smirked. Perfumed oil teased my nose—probably her hair was soft with it. Her robe was plain white linen with much wear about the hem but she looked at me so pert and frank I was eager to push her down and go in her right then. And I think I would've had not some of the village women interrupted us and shooed me off.—You'll get your chance soon enough they laughed at us both—steering Huneisha away and swatting her bottom. How I longed to be one of those old crones at that moment with their knobby hands slapping her there.

—Soon enough! they laughed.

They were wrong in the end.

So it was that I spent the time waiting for things to happen. For other people to make arrangements as to how my life would proceed. How often this occurs in the course of our days—we think we are in charge when really we are anything but. Merely passive observers in our lives that others decide how best to control.

And how fiercely we pretend otherwise.

At times I wandered along the path out of the village heading west towards the sea. The coast was many miles away but my mind often turned towards the great Philistine cities of Hebron and Jaffa and wondered what they were like. And the sea beyond. And thus preoccupied I would return to the village by way of the olive groves or else the vineyard where I had met the lion. One day in so doing I discovered a singular thing.

Without realizing it I had entered that same path where I had been attacked and lo! what should I see but the lion's head on the ground tilted at me frothing and writhing as if it had come back to life. I admit to being plenty scared by this but forcing myself closer I soon laughed aloud at my skittishness. For the lion's head had no more come to life than stone or sword or clay pot but it was filled with a multitude of honeybees which swarmed in and out of its mouth past its fangs standing like sentries to guard the entrance to some heathen shrine. A steady stream of insects it was too and well did I know what they'd be busy making—for if there's one thing that can be said about honeybees it's that their industry is a model for all of God's lesser creatures and not a few of His higher ones as well.

So I waved the swarm aside and reached past the frozen fangs of the lion and broke off as big a chunk of honeycomb as I could manage. The insects harried me furiously but I fear no living creature and waved my hand to create a whirlwind and drove them back. And if any did sting me they were too puny to notice and died in their folly.

The honey was sweet and warm in my mouth as the wax melted greasily to slide down my throat. My whole being was suffused with the odor and flavor of flowers. I will confess to being inordinately fond of sweet things and honey most of all. As vices go this strikes me as a small one.

A few stray insects harassed me for a time before giving up to return to their hive. I strolled on beneath the afternoon summer sun with my mouth full of honey and my wife-to-be waiting for me with her (I imagined) wet loins and life was very sweet indeed.

My parents met me when I returned to the small hut that had been set aside for my use. Manue my father said—The feast is arranged for tomorrow. It will last seven days and at the end of it you'll be a husband.

This pleased me well.

Sala my mother took my hand and said—We are happy for you my child. Huneisha seems a sweet girl and shall make a fine wife.

—You have no more reservations then?

—None that matter said my father.

This pleased me even better. I shared with them the honeycomb and we all sat eating and smiling at one another. For a time the three of us all felt very contented. Soon of course would come the bitterness & disillusionment pain & blood slaughter & fear but for that night there was just sweetness and joy melting waxily across our tongues.

The Riddle

The next day I put on my fine tunic of new linen. Some of the infidel women wove me a garland of violets and clover and led me to the home of Huneisha's father. Tables had been set up in long rows. There was to be a mighty wedding feast of lamb & mutton goat & pig (it pained me to see this but they were Philistines after all) kidneys & tongue and bread both wheat & barley and soups of barley & lentil and great piles of apricots & grapes figs & honey cakes for later. And of course as much wine as could be bought for though I was a Nazirite the same couldn't be said for my wife's family or village nor for that matter my own. Judging by the abundance of ceramic urns lining the yard there would be no shortage.

The whole of Thamnatha was there as well as many of my aunts and some other guests from my village of Dan. Although generally the Philistines kept to one side and my people kept to themselves there was a degree of mingling and conviviality and shared goodwill. At the risk of sounding immodest again I think it was myself and Huneisha who were responsible for much of this as we were after all forging a bond between our peoples for all to see. On top of this was her father who extended every courtesy to both me and my parents and he labored to make this consideration evident. At any other time I'd've said he was a braggart or a man whose flaunting of his good intentions left them hollow—but in this particular case he might have been forgiven as after all the situation was far from ordinary.

He was built something like a spider but jolly enough in his way with a white-flecked beard and a habit of leaning into you whenever he spoke as if forever delivering a message of the strictest confidence. Because he was bald and his scalp was covered with an array of spots and knobs this habit of leaning close could be unnerving. My eye tended to fall upon those blemishes and I wondered what they signified. He sat to my left at the head of the first table with my own parents to my right and Huneisha at another table with some women. The rest of my table was given over to my thirty companions: men of roughly my age whom the villagers had appointed as special caretakers for me seeing as I was new to the village and unschooled in their customs. Such was the tradition of the Philistines when an outsider married into the village and I must say it was a custom that reflected well on them.

We feasted and drank and they grew sloppy and bantered much and generally made me feel welcome which I appreciated. I will admit to drinking a small amount of wine as well to show my new comrades that I was their brother for so they urged and I admit the sweet taste pleased me well. Certainly though it was Devil's drink for it induced all manner of foolish thoughts and much overly loud laughter. Manue and Sala sent many sharp glances in my direction but I ignored them. For indeed I was concentrating on my thirty companions and wished for something to show them my goodwill. So I had an idea (or perhaps the Devil having one spoke through the wine) and said to them:—Would you have a riddle?

This was a custom of my people done at times of celebration. For all I knew the Philistines did so too although gauging from their expressions of bewilderment this was not the case.

—What's this? they demanded.—What did you say?

—A riddle I repeated.

Still they looked baffled and I will admit to a fledgling uncertainty. Perhaps this was something best left aside for now. But I felt also that this hand of fellowship had been extended and to pull it back now would be an act of provocation if not outright belligerence. Helplessly I looked at my father who watched the proceedings under a heavy brow. And he said— Listen then all of you. Among the Israelites it is common to play such games at festive moments like this. But it is nothing to be taken overly seriously and if you wish let it pass there's no harm to it.

The companions protested vigorously and Huneisha's father cackled and cried:—Too late to back out now! Let's have it.

And the men pounded the table till the cups rattled and sloshed.—Yes! Yes!

More than once in my life I have looked back at this moment and wondered if I should have considered more carefully before speaking aloud. But the feast was so jovial and my parents so richly honored and Huneisha so ripe in her clean linen with a garland of chamomile flowers tucked through her hair and the kohl applied to make her eyes even deeper and more startling that I felt the need to prolong the good feeling and enrich it. I shall go to my grave protesting that there was nothing more than this that prompted my tongue.

So I said to them—Here is my riddle for the thirty of you my companions. If you solve it I will give to each of you a new tunic and cloak.

At this they raised their cups and hurrahed.

—But if you don't solve it I warned—you must give me each of you a tunic and cloak so that makes thirty altogether.

Much laughter followed this and they agreed. Doubtless they thought the thirty of them would make short work of any one man's puzzle. And under ordinary circumstances they'd have been right. But I had a riddle that none knew the answer to save me.

Would that I never spoke it.

I said—Hear then: Out of the eater came forth meat and out of the strong came forth sweetness. Now solve that riddle.

And the thirty companions looked at one another and looked at me and said:—Heh?

So I repeated it. The whole gathering had gone hushed and my words rang clear like chimes. So too the wine helped me speak loudly and—as I thought—with unaccustomed clarity.—Out of the eater came forth meat I said.—And out of the strong came forth sweetness. That's my riddle for you all my companions.

There were many empty looks and furrowed brows so I happily resumed eating thinking expectantly of the unforeseen bounty of tunics and cloaks I was to receive. And as I ate and drank I spoke quietly to Huneisha's father and didn't notice at that time how little he spoke in return. Nor did I notice the lowered brows dark looks and unhappy glowering glances that were turned my way by my own guests on the first day of my wedding feast.

Not till later did I remember and wonder at them but by then it was far too late.

The Answer to the Riddle

For three days the feast went on. My companions showered many forced smiles and meaningless toasts upon me and Huneisha but they grew no closer to solving the riddle. Over time their jests grew more bitter and their smiles more dishonest. But complacent as I was I ignored the tension running below the surface like an underground river and simply took delight at their outlandish guesses:

—The eater is the pig and the meat is pork!

—What then is the sweetness? Its offal?

—Wait—listen—the strong is woman for she bears the pain of her confinement. And the sweetness she brings forth is her child.

—And I suppose the child is meat too? Or maybe her afterbirth!

This was met with great gusts of laughter.

—All right then try this. The eater is the bullock. Why do I say this? Because it eats grass as we all know. Yet we slaughter it for meat—and no man will deny its strength. That's three of the clues then.

—Very well. And the fourth? The sweetness?

—I leave that to you.

Again the laughter. But as days passed four five six and the seventh approached my companions began to worry lest they had after all to provide me with garments beyond their expectation or perhaps even their means. And if I noticed during this time that my bride Huneisha badgered me unduly for the answer to the riddle—well I never troubled myself about it preferring to imagine her caught up in the excitement of the thing.

—Tell me! she wheedled in my ear with more urgency each day.—Tell me the answer as you love me.

—How can I tell you? Even my parents don't know.

Her sulks grew extreme but this only made her more fetching than ever.—You don't love me then she accused.—You'd trust me if you did. And she looked so upset as she said these words that I wondered if she really believed it.

—Oh hush now I said but this seemed the wrong answer. I will admit that I had little experience coaxing smiles from women—usually they came easily enough with no urging. But Huneisha seemed unresponsive to whatever charms I could muster and briefly I wondered whether this was a portent of our future life together.

Of course there was more taking place than I knew because she hadn't told me and it was this: the men of her village had pulled her aside and weren't gentle about it. She should've come to me and explained but maybe she feared for me or more likely for them as there were only thirty and she thought their lives would be forfeit if I learned of their harsh treatment. (She was of course right.) In any event she didn't tell me what was going on and I didn't learn till later by which time events had come and gone. Another man might grieve for her but I reckon that what came to her was a fair recompense for not taking her husband into confidence.

They pulled her aside and said—Find out the answer to this damned riddle.

—And how am I supposed to do that? demanded Huneisha with a feisty tilt of her chin.

They grabbed her elbow and shook it and the men circled round her like wild dogs.—You figure something out they said.—What do you think—that we came to your wedding to show ourselves as fools and paupers? You do as we say or else.

—Or else what?

—Or else you die. Understand? We shall come in the night to torch your father's house with you still in it and your parents as well. Your husband will be left alive to mourn for the rest of his life.

So she came to me and wept with great drama. As I say I didn't know any of this but she carried on so pathetically it grew more than a little annoying. This was our wedding after all not the birth of our stillborn child nor the aftermath of some battle that left our families dead. And I defy any man to sit only a few paces from his bride at his wedding celebration with her cheeks slick with tears and the kohl smudged into tracks running in vertical lines beneath her eyes and her head bent low like some cur that's been kicked. I defy any man to look at that and think to himself: *All is as it should be praise the LORD.* Maybe you're the man to do it but I'm not. So bear that in mind as I tell this tale before you pass your judgment as I know you will.

On the morning of the seventh day I awoke weary of her tears and determined to make things right so I called for the women to bring her and then led her a little ways off and revealed the answer to the riddle. My heart was so troubled I could do nothing else and happy I was to have done it—for she wiped her face clean and smiled at me before promising pleasure beyond all ordinary experience that evening. Our first together as man and wife.

This thought had been much on my mind of late. Satisfied that the matter was done I retired after breakfast much preoccupied with my mind's picture of my new bride and fretting not at all about the riddle.

It was too good to last. Returning to the feast at midday I found everyone awaiting me and my thirty Philistine so-called brothers wearing the sleepy-eyed contented expressions of kittens recently fed. One of them was round-faced and slope-shouldered and would've been called big standing beside anyone but me. His name was Baal which as it happens is the name of one of the heathen's gods as well. Maybe this fact had affected his personality from a young age for humble he was not. Upon seeing me approach the table he called out—Lo! Is this a lion that approaches? He's certainly got the hair for it!

Among his companions there burst a cacophony of cackles and hoots. My step slowed as of its own will till it stopped entirely behind the seat of my bride Huneisha. It's likely my hands balled themselves tight into fists at this moment but if so it's nothing I did with any degree of awareness.

Baal drawled on—What is stronger than a lion? And yet

when the lion is slain it's nothing more than meat like any other carcass.

—Very true! called out some in the crowd.—And very clever too! Go on Baal—tell us about the sweetness.

—Nothing simpler. Baal smiled. His grin was broad and made his round face even rounder. It occurred to me that Baal was the kind of large man who liked to be the center of things and maybe he'd taken it hard that attention this past week had been on me. But if there was any truth to this speculation it hadn't come in time to do me any good. Now Baal said—As for sweetness—what's sweeter than honey? And if the honey should come from a hive in the dead lion's mouth what's that but strength bringing forth sweetness?

Somehow my fingers had gotten entwined in Huneisha's hair. The strands lay fine and feathery against my skin and as gentle as her breath. She herself sat completely rigid as I passed my hand through the strands and lifted them to my nose: oil. Oil and roses.

They were all watching me.—You'd not know that riddle without plowing with my heifer I said.

At this some of them looked confused or even a little startled.—We've not touched her declared one while another growled—And you'd be safer not making such accusations.

To which there was a great deal of vigorous nodding and even more vigorous frowning and adjusting of loins.

—I'm not saying anyone's lain with her I said. And this was true too for if I'd thought that then all these companions would've been cold already and stiffening in the dirt.—I mean only that you couldn't know the answer to my riddle without taking undue advantage of my position here as a stranger among you all.

—But know it we do smirked Baal and again there was much nodding among the others. They were of course all drunk and had been for days and would have happily nodded to just about anything. Baal said—Your accusation is empty but you seem intent on reneging on your promise. So much— and here he raised his voice to address the whole assembly—so much for Israelite promises. We should have known better.

My father stiffened in his chair and Huneisha's father snapped—You watch your tongue. Samson is our guest. As are his kin and countrymen.

All the villagers of Dan had grown taut & silent watchful & stern.

Baal shrugged elaborately and his lackeys agreed with this as well.

—Pay him no mind I declared to them all. To Baal I said:—You've solved the riddle so fear not. You'll get your re- ward. After all—I can see why a new tunic would mean a lot to such as you.

Baal scowled but had no reply.

Looking upon his thick stupid face then I reflected on Huneisha's betrayal—for there was no other word for it—and the duplicity of my so-called companions. My mind grew sluggish with the unfairness of it and it grew hard to think. And I won- dered then for a moment if my parents hadn't been right after all: if it was a mistake to pursue this union with a Philistine girl. Well too late now. But in my heart I came upon a plan to teach these wretches a thing or two about Israelite promises. For I was a part of their lives now even as they were a part of mine. If they wished to deceive & mock dishonor & spoil then they should know that I was as skilled at those arts as any of them. Yes I would teach them this and it was to be a lesson they'd not soon forget.

My thoughts came a little clearer when I had decided on my path.—Which is the nearest village? I asked.

—Ascalon answered several of them.—A village of our brother Philistines.

This suited me well. I said—Where is it and how far and how large?

They pointed west.—Half a day's walk they said and perhaps sixty families. But it's not a market town. You might barter for a few garments but not enough.

There was no point answering. A strange calmness had fallen upon me and I knew the LORD was with me again as He had been when I faced the lion. And as with the lion I knew He would stay with me till the fight was done.

The crowd was watching me as they might look upon a child who's just received an unwelcome surprise of no great import to anyone but him. I said to them—Nobody leave. I will be back by morning with your things.

Baal's face was round and empty as he said—You're going right now?

This question was so stupid I simply turned and left.

Ascalon

Arriving at Ascalon at dusk I found that it had been described truly.

Two men were returning from the fields on the path ahead of me carrying scythes over their shoulders. They waited as I hailed them and drew near. I wrung the neck of the first like a chicken and he died without a word.

The second said—What are you—and I sliced his throat

with his companion's scythe. Quickly I stripped the shirts and cloaks from these men and piled them behind a distinctive boulder alongside the path. The bodies went into a gully. A little farther along I came across a man with three grown sons laboring in their wheat. One son marked my approach and said—Peace stranger and I crushed his windpipe with the flat of my hand. He took some time to die but he was the third.

The fourth was the father who howled at me and swung a hoe at my head. I snapped it in two and impaled the man on the sharp split.

Truly the LORD was with me that night.

The fifth said—Mercy please! and I staved in his head with a rock.

The sixth was a tear-streaked boy who said—For the sake of my mother don't kill all of us and I wrenched his head as I had the lion's. The four bodies I left where they fell while their garments went with the others.

Farther on I happened upon a man voiding his bowels in the brush. He said—You come to watch? and I throttled him with a length of vine. He was the seventh.

The eighth sat in his workshop a little ways outside the village sharpening his sword on a whetstone. When I said—The blade appears dull yet he handed the weapon to me saying—See for yourself so I hacked his neck to the bone.

The ninth sat in the next hut along scraping the fat off a fleece.—Damn filthy animals he said cheerfully and I pushed his face into the fur until his body convulsed and stilled.

The tenth was watching from the doorway when I turned around. He said—Please no as I punched as hard as I could with the heel of my hand into his nose.

I piled those bodies in the hut and made my way to the village center where some sort of gathering was in progress—a criminal proceeding it appeared. I approached unmarked and tapped one man on the shoulder and he said—Shhh so I pulled him aside and wrapped my hand over his face and he never shushed anyone again. He was the eleventh. But this didn't go unnoticed and suddenly I was at the center of a howling mob of Philistines. Fortunately the calmness and serenity of the LORD's peace beat within my bosom so I was able to slaughter my enemies with speed and unconcern. And so does the One True God show His clemency and love to those who but strive to carry out His wishes with a pure heart.

The twelfth was a hairy brute who wielded a loaf of bread as though it were a powerful club. He said—What devil has sent you among us? and I rammed the bread into his throat and left him to choke upon it.

The thirteenth and fourteenth together rushed me screeching some incoherent babble and I seized their heads like melons and slammed them together and let them drop. Like melons they broke and leaked away into the dust.

The fifteenth was an old man crooked and bent standing beside the firepit who gazed at me with watery eyes above a white beard and said—You wouldn't harm an old man would you? and I knocked him backwards into the fire to roast like the pig he was.

The sixteenth was the bound prisoner whose testimony the others had been hearing upon my arrival. He smiled at me and said—Friend I like your style—now free me and let's be off. So I took his bound wrists and tore the ropes loose before binding them round his neck and tossing him over a tree to hang kicking till he kicked no longer. One thing I know for certain is that the LORD didn't place me in this world to pass my time with criminals.

The seventeenth came at me with an ax and I hacked off his legs and left him to drain.

The eighteenth was a youth with more courage than sense who faced me with a sling as he cried out—You don't scare me! I tore the sling from his sweaty hand and used it on him till he lay flat and cooling.

The nineteenth leapt upon me from behind with a knife. I hurled him from me and into the twentieth snapping both their necks. Then I caught up the twenty-first and used the knife to cleave him from neck to kidneys. That one I had to disrobe quickly for there was such a quantity of blood it would've rendered the garments quite unwearable. Killing thirty men was enough of a task: I had no desire to hunt up yet more simply for their clothes.

The villagers no longer fought but turned to flee. All but one who sat quietly in the village clearing with such a placid look on his face I almost took him for dead already till he said to me—I know not why you've brought such hatred and pain but let me offer my life in exchange for the village. There was nothing to say to such stupidity so I kicked the fool's head flat and left him there while I pursued the others. That was twenty-two.

The twenty-third begged for mercy till I staved in his lungs and ended his begging.

The twenty-fourth stood tall and proud and silent as if to impress me. I put out his eyes with my thumbs and broke his skull with a stout branch.

The twenty-fifth hollered—You'll not catch me! and ran like a gazelle till I forced him over a cliff and then he ran no farther.

The twenty-sixth hid in a stable with a number of asses so I panicked the animals and they kicked and bucked and reared and did the work of killing him for me. He might've said something but I don't know what for the asses drowned out his efforts.

The twenty-seventh was fat. Flushed and sweating he offered me riches and women till he collapsed of his own fear and weak heart.

The twenty-eighth twisted his ankle in flight and sprawled on the earth. Looking up at me he held out his hands and begged—Don't hit me. I said—All right and instead fell upon him with all my weight.

The twenty-ninth was the hardest because he had run into the river and hid beneath the water. It took me some time to find him and wade out but once I did his witless thrashing made it easy to follow. His head was underwater while I clenched it below the surface so there was nothing to hear of his final words but the sudden uprush of bubbles breaking the surface.

The thirtieth was a young man cowering in a cave who said—Please don't kill me for I'm soon to be married.

I said—As am I and was done with it.

So then. Thirty men lay dead and if there were others in this village they had scattered in cowardice. The women and children had either fled as well or lay terrified in their huts but this was no concern of mine: it was not my business to kill innocents.

Some moments passed as I caught my breath and wiped the sweat from my eyes and waited for my heart to slow to its usual pace. Dark had come by now and I was mightily tired as you can imagine but still I had to strip the bodies & collect the garments into a pile bind them up & make my way by moonlight back to Thamnatha. This I duly did. Along the way I reflected on my father Manue's advice about one's final words and wondered what he would've made of the many I had heard that night. None stood out as especially memorable.

Just after dawn I arrived at Thamnatha to find my thirty companions still carousing and carrying on.

They fell silent at my approach but spying the heap of clothes in my arms grew excited again. I dropped the garments on the ground and the men squabbled and hissed for the choicest pieces as avidly as any flock of women. They didn't mind that many of the garments were torn in places or wet with mud and blood or sporting fresh rents or tatters. Indeed the men were so giddy with wine and their late night and their own satisfaction at besting me that they seemed to notice these things not at all.

A great weariness and disgust rose up in me seeing them like that. The calm of the LORD had long gone and my parents were abed and the women including Huneisha were nowhere in sight. I was truly married now but felt nothing—neither joy nor desire nor any other healthy human feeling. Even if my wife was waiting ready for me I was too tired and bitter to take her as a husband should. So instead I turned back up the path towards my village some three days' walk to the east. I could barely keep myself erect: my legs were weak after my night's exertions and it seemed a long time before the hoots and laughter of the festivities faded behind me.

What Huneisha Did

Who can understand a woman's mind? Its baffling irrationality and rejection of all sense? Not me and believe it I've tried. Perhaps I've just had bad luck with Huneisha & Dalila and the rest but often it seems to me that the woman hasn't yet lived who possesses clear thinking and logic to any significant degree with one exception. That of course being my dear mother Sala.

What happened was this. I was delayed in returning to Thamnatha for some weeks because of one crisis or another. As the only son of my parents there was always a need. Finally the harvest came and I was required to reap & thresh winnow & store the grain after digging out and expanding the silos. At last I was free to return to Thamnatha although knowing what awaited me there it would've been best if I had stayed under my parents' roof forever.

For when I met Huneisha's father he looked most perplexed and more than slightly fearful.—Lo then child why are you here?

A more baffling question I couldn't have easily imagined. I said—I'm here to have my wife or have you forgotten our seven-day feast?

He looked away sidewards and crept a little closer as was his wont. For this I got another fine view of the landscape of his scalp. Leaning towards me as if we were conspirators he said— I thought you'd taken it into your head that you hated her and chose to spurn her forever.

—And why should I do that?

—Well the whole business of the riddle for one thing.

And then Huneisha's father revealed to me what had happened with my wedding companions and the threats they had made. This news didn't sit well with me but at least I better understood Huneisha's actions. But before I could resolve on a future course her father went on:—Then you disappeared and next thing we know you're back in your family's home and my daughter is left abandoned spurned and weeping.

To myself I thought *Weeping is something I didn't know she was so partial to* but I didn't say this aloud. Instead I said only—I had my reasons for what I did.

He straightened up.—That's as may be he said.—What's done is done. Then he leaned close again.—But you understand I've got my honor to think of and hers. She had a wedding so she needed a husband and you weren't there. A terrible bind it was for the both of us. Surely you can see that?

I didn't like this conversation so I said nothing.

—Since her husband was gone I had to find her another. Huneisha's father spread his spidery arms wide. His hands were deep-lined with muddy tracks that would never wash clean no matter how hard he scrubbed and his fingers looked long and thin enough to snap off like pea pods. He said—So I gave her another one.

No I didn't like this conversation at all.

—Are you listening? He frowned.

—You're saying I said—you're saying you gave my wife to another man and he's had her and gone in. You're saying that.

—I'm saying he said—your wife chose another man as her husband when the husband she thought she had decided to leave her and never came back.

Calmness settled over me like a thick fleece across my shoulders. It dampened not my fury but merely controlled it—held it back momentarily so it could be channeled into a more useful canal of violence and destruction.

—Are they here? I asked.

—No he said.—They've gone back to Baal's village.

This struck me like a blow.

—But listen he said—she has a sister don't despair. Younger yes and prettier too—fairer of skin and better shaped with more of what she needs to give you sons. You know? More of what *you* need as well. Man to man—he leaned towards me closer than ever and waved at the air with his pea-pod fingers—Huneisha takes after me while this other favors her mother.

The calmness was still there but I felt a buzzing rattle through my head as if that honey I had eaten all those weeks ago had carried grubs that were even now transforming themselves into a swarm that raged through me like vengeance. Ignoring the words of Huneisha's father I said—You have done me great wrong all of you. Have you already forgotten what happened at Ascalon?

At this he looked worried as well he might. As well he might. News of the slaughter had spread far by this time. He said— Well let's not—

—Listen I said.—You've wronged me beyond all measure and you will be repaid. That's a vow you'd best believe. And not just this village either but the whole nation of Philistines shall bear my vengeance and be witness to it.

—That's a little much isn't it? Just for a girl? I mean— daughter or no—one's much the same as the next after all. I'm the first to admit—

I shut him up by putting my hand across his mouth and he dared not lift his own hand against me. There were by now quite a number of villagers gathered nearby and more faces in doorways and windows. Several familiar guests from my wedding but that was over and counted as nothing so I would not let myself be swayed. To the crowd I spoke and my voice was strong and loud and did not waver. I said—Understand this. From this day forth I am at war with the Philistines. Any of you is my enemy. Do not resist my wrath: the best you can do

is flee from it. For I will do evils to you unlike any you have
imagined before. Curse me all you wish but remember that I
am blameless in all my actions for you yourselves have brought
us to this pass.

I left the village then and they said nothing as I went which
suited me fine. After all what could they say? Ascalon had been
only a beginning I saw that now. Soon they would see it too.
Soon the entire Philistine nation would be Ascalon. They
would come to know the full extent of the LORD's fury. And
my own.

What I Did

Many days have passed while I remain enchained here
in Dagon's temple and I have had much to reflect on. No less
than my whole life in fact. I doze and wake and doze again and
upon waking this last time I have found that my sight has
nearly left me altogether. I can barely see anything at all in this
range of gray and shadows: the huge firepit that burns in the
center of it all is no more than a dull red spot like the nub of
bronze in the fire. Surely I am but half a step away from total
helplessness yet I will not complain because I am sustained by
the LORD in this as in all things.

My other senses continue to work if anything more acutely
than before. Thus I feel the weight of the shackles so fiercely
I'm tempted to cry out. I smell the smoldering fire and taste the
acid bile rising from my gut. Most of all I hear the perverse
laughter and sibilant murmurings of the Philistines as they
range themselves about me engaging in every sinful practice
imaginable—especially the ones that come most readily to

mind. Yes even those they carry out but a few paces from me and they call it worship. Dagon their god may be half-man half-fish but truly his followers engage in things I've never heard of done before by any man nor any fish either.

The priest Meth or Menth comes and goes as well. He seems almost drawn to me—as if my presence here is some conundrum for him to resolve but which forever eludes him.

But enough of all that. To distract myself I will tell of what I did when Huneisha proved herself a harlot and took another man inside as her husband.

For some days I thought and planned and nothing more. When I was done thinking I set out to capture a fox and then another and then several others. At which point I saw no reason to pause and by the time I was finished I had three hundred beasts contained in pens & baskets deep pits & tied in chains. Probably you have never captured even a single fox so you doubt my ability to trap so many. Trust me it's true. There are tricks and I used them all—baiting my snares with hens & kids lambs & even fox pups. Plus I took advantage of that strange sympathy I can exert over animals which I have mentioned before now. Once the beasts were in my snares I was quick to leap upon them and you already know that I fear no beast alive. And it's a good thing too or I'd've had a terrible time tying their tails together and setting them all on fire.

Probably this is something else you've never done and I wouldn't advise it. It's difficult enough binding one tail to the next while each animal writhes and snarls and fights to bolt off in the opposite direction and I admit to losing a few this way. But that inconvenience was nothing compared to their madness when they saw me bearing the flaming timber and squatting beside them for then they lurched into the sky twisting like airborne creatures and emitting such noises as would make a demon shudder. I admit to setting the creatures aflame quickly and stepping away in relief when it was done.

Despite my best precautions I nearly set my own beard alight on more than one occasion.

What happens of course when an animal is set on fire is that it runs wildly in all directions spreading mayhem. When another creature is bound to it the chaos increases manifold. And when a hundred fifty (minus the few I had lost) such pairs are set aflame and released there is then created such a profusion of havoc that is gratifying indeed to witness.

The Philistine fields were nearby and this was no accident. Because their farms are found lower down than the mountainous villages of my people their season is longer and harvest comes later. Thus some of the wheat was yet standing while the rest had been gathered into great mounds dotting the countryside. By this time it was tinder dry and when the foxes tore through it like bolts of lightning laid sideways on the ground the whole landscape erupted into inferno. Not only the heaped sheaves but the standing grain was soon reduced to smoldering ash and the silage that had been cut for the animals as well. And still the foxes flew onward—those who were still alive—through the vineyards and olive groves where many collapsed among the trees and soon plumes of smoke could be seen rising from them. Those plumes quickly turned to a thick foggy blanket as every olive tree was devoured and every grapevine shriveled like the fur on a burning fox's back.

By now all the animals were burnt and dead but they'd served their purpose and I wished them well. I know our teachers say that animals do not pass into the next life but still I hoped that some would so that after my own death I might meet them there and thank them for their service.

Men from the Philistine villages tried to douse the flames but a breeze had kicked up favorable to my task and the smoke billowed low across the countryside driving the fools back. It hunkered like a living thing and seemed ready to reach out and swat any heathen who approached carrying an urn of water to save some precious tree or vine. And in this way it became clear that the whole region was lost or more properly had been made a holocaust or burnt offering unto the LORD.

Chaos ruled over the landscape. If the Philistines had remained calm and worked together they could have saved much. But they did neither: they ran helter-skelter like a nest of ants that's been kicked—creating so much havoc that here a minor fire was allowed to grow into an inferno and there a few panicked animals swelled into a stampede that left whole villages bereft of livestock. One man's loss lurched and bumped into the next man's and the next until before long the destruction had spread beyond all comprehending. The very landscape looked as though an army had passed through the region not just a few fiery animals. And from this I learned a valuable lesson: that it takes only a modest amount of disruption to create an inordinate amount of mayhem. It's not necessary to wreak all the destruction yourself. Just begin with a fair amount and man's stupidity and selfishness will do the rest.

After this I waited to see what would happen.

What the Philistines Did

What the Philistines did was take revenge on the whore Huneisha and her father by going to their homes and burning them to cinders. I suppose the whore's pimp Baal died too but I never heard. Then word was sent to me saying that vengeance had been extracted upon those who had wronged me. An appeal for peace was made: things said about putting this unfortunate incident behind us and so on. This was done I suppose in hopes of placating my anger which just shows that the only thing stupider than a Philistine is a whole crowd of Philistines.

The envoy they sent was an Edomite and I had no argument with him. I said—Tell them I'm not done with my revenge and I won't be silent till I finish.

The Edomite went away and I waited. Avoiding my own village of Dan—for I didn't want trouble to follow me there—I kept to the hills between the Philistines and my people. I knew that if I waited long enough they would come to find me for fear wouldn't let them stay away but I knew also that there would be a period of confusion argument and indecision. About both these things I was right.

How many I slaughtered when they came for me at last I can't say. Scores at least or maybe hundreds. It was like Ascalon again only more so. My enemies stood before me like blades of grass in a field and I cut them down as with a scythe. It took all of a day and a night and part of the next day and when I stopped the sandy earth was red mud and pieces and piles of dead things lay everywhere. Only maybe a dozen men survived and I let them flee to spread word of what had happened and with this the fear. For I wanted the fear to spread among the Philistines and take root and grow strong and tall and unshakeable like the mightiest cedar tree ever. And after this I knew I must leave my home behind so I traveled north into unfamiliar hills till I came to a cavern near Etam. I didn't know the name at the time but I do now and I squatted there and waited and occasionally hunted or bathed in the river all the while waiting to see what course of action the Philistines would decide upon. For now I had well and truly declared war upon the whole nation of them and this couldn't be ignored. And to those who would say that I did nothing but sit and wait in those days I would answer: Making war against an entire people is no small business and nothing to bluster away at thoughtlessly. The wise man knows the time for action as well as calm and though I make no claim to being a wise man it was obvious even to me that I couldn't go around forever bashing the skulls of my enemies without some time given over to thought and reflection.

I feared not however for I had the LORD to guide my hand and guide it He would. My cause was just and I had broken no law so my conscience was as clear as the day my beloved mother had birthed me.

The season passed. Harvests were gathered and winter came on. Things were happening that I wouldn't learn of till later. Foremost among these things was the raising of a vast army of Philistines numbering in the thousands. This force swept across the land subjugating my people's villages and imposing their laws. Many brave men resisted and were killed but many more capitulated eagerly and were soon indistinguishable from the enemy themselves. For such is the way of my people as I have lamented before. We are a brave race but often forget our courage along with our devotion to the LORD. We are quick to adopt the habits of those around us—whether from genuine desire or simple laziness or maybe a misguided sense of self-preservation I couldn't say.

Before long the army had encamped at a place called Lechi which some men call the Jawbone. It's a narrow valley bent as the name suggests and not a good spot for an uneven battle since the army's advantage of greater numbers would be nullified by the constricted space. But the Philistines have always been laughably poor strategists and besides they never had any notion of battling me. Rather they thought to impress me with their numbers and so overpower me without a fight. Well good luck to them.

What happened was this. Envoys were sent to my own people, those of the tribe of Juda. And because of a desire to avoid bloodshed or the belief that they couldn't overwhelm that army of thousands or because of simple cowardice the tribe of Juda consented to the heathens' demand which was:— Go to your wayward brother Samson and bind him and bring him to us.

Being heathen already in their hearts these so-called men willingly consented but being yet more afraid of their own brother than their declared enemy they made sure to bring a force of three thousand to subdue me.

The weather had turned bitter by then. My breath flowed white before me in the chill as I sat on a boulder and watched them approach. An army of that size does nothing by stealth and as they descended from the hills I could have easily slipped away but there was no point. I was tired of waiting and felt the time of action had arrived one way or another and besides was curious to hear what my brothers had to say. For all I knew this could be a force of men coming to pledge their swords to mine to overthrow the invader and drive him from the land once and for all just as our ancestor Josue had done so many years before.

Alas no. Upon seeing me their advance scouts halted and laid their weapons upon the ground and I showed my empty hands and did not move from my seat. The scouts ran back to find their I supposed leaders. I waited yet more. Long thin afternoon shadows fell through the trees and the air cooled even further in advance of the approaching night. This was the time of day when birds were at their chattiest yet today they'd all scattered in the face of the approaching army.

The elders arrived and sat upon boulders facing me and said without preamble—You know why we are here.

Actually I didn't and I said as much.

The frailest-looking of the elders had massive brows and a surprisingly sharp voice.—The Philistines have grown so enraged at your ill treatment he said—that they have taken revenge over all our people. Yea even your own village of Dan is not spared.

And hearing these words I felt deeply grieved. As I said before I had moved from the region of my birth to avoid just this calamity but it was for naught. Scarcely had I time to take this in before the elders were demanding—What has made you act so? Why have you done this when you knew how they'd respond?

I had no answer other than the truth which was that I thought fear would make them cautious. But then no one could ever predict how a Philistine would respond to any situation and for proof of that look no further than my alleged wife Huneisha. Still the aggression of the Philistine response was a surprise—but saying as much aloud would have left me looking ignorant and unworldly. So I said only:—As they have done to me so I have done to them.

Great windy exhalations and a reshuffling of backsides greeted this. Maybe this was because the stones burned cold through the old men's linens but maybe there was another reason. Finally one of the men said—My son you have slain many of them but nobody ever threatened to slay you.

—They have slain my honor I said.

—Yes but you have murdered their menfolk.

—They have murdered my honor.

—Many of their wives face starvation and their children lie dying already from famine or pestilence.

—Just as my honor has been taken from me I said.—Don't blame me for the pestilence in any case for I'm not to blame for that. Though it's true enough that I would visit it upon them if I could.

More weighty sighs met this but I trusted I had made my point.

Then the eldest of the elders slapped his knees and said—Listen then. We have come not to talk but to bind you and transport you as prisoner to the Philistines. Much discussion we have given over to this topic and that is our decision. Now will you come quietly or is it your wish to wage war against your own people along with the heathen?

I turned this over in my mind. It was a bitter stew in my mouth to be betrayed by Israelites—by the tribe of Juda no less—but not wholly unexpected. And mixed with the pain and disappointment of betrayal was the glimmering of what I might do against the enemy once I was brought among them. I could be as a fox running aflame through their fields. Truly it was as if the LORD Himself stood beside me and placed His hand on my shoulder and bent towards me to whisper—Fret ye not all will be well. And feeling those words in my heart I knew any obstacle could be overcome and there was nothing to fear.

—Promise me one thing I said.—That you will not kill me.

Many heads nodded vigorously.—It's not our charge to kill you said the elder.—Only to bind you and take you to the Philistines.

—Who will then kill me I said.—Or try.

They wouldn't meet my eye.—That is between you and them. Who would have believed my people to be such cowards?

I stood and held out my wrists.—Tie me I said—and use the stoutest cords you have so none may later accuse you of treachery.

And so they did. And the ropes lay against my flesh like the harlot Huneisha's hair and I knew they would snap just as easily. But I hung my head and pretended that they had bound me as fast as the stoutest manacles of iron.

Jawbone

It was a dry and dusty place they took me to. This Jawbone.

Very briefly let me describe the land more carefully than I have so far. My people live in a series of small villages and towns along the ridge of hills running like a spine through the heart of Canaan. To the east range the great deserts of the Edomites and Ammonites and other nomads and to the west lie the fertile plateau of the Philistines and beyond that the sea. Mixed in with the Philistines are the Canaanites and other tribes that hold themselves separate from the Israelites and us from them and godless heathens are they all. Many leagues south lies Goshen the land of Pharoah where my people were enslaved not so many generations ago and to the north lies much arid land and then the lush green valleys of the Tigris and Euphrates. From here come the periodic tiresome attacks by Akkadians as well as other tribes of fierce warriors who like locusts swarm southward at intervals when they grow tired of living peaceful and contented lives. And of course from there too came Abram later Abraham the father of Isaac father of Jacob and so ancestor to all those tribes who identify themselves as Israelites.

Now I was brought to the very northernmost tip of my people's land where the wind blows parched off the desert and the western plains carry only a hint of their abundant fertility. Here a steep ravine cuts into the plateau and twists sharply into an elongated L shape. This is Lechi called also Jawbone and here I was transported and delivered unto the hosts of mine enemies.

How many enemies? Well the Israelites brought three thousand just to bear me there and the Philistines had no less. I will leave you to imagine the number.

We marched through the night and arrived at dawn. My companions were exhausted by their effort and by the cold but for my part I had been resting for weeks and felt strong. The Israelites led me down to the floor of the ravine and then swiftly left. I didn't see money change hands but wouldn't've been surprised to. (Another weakness of my people or perhaps I should say of every people: the power that mammon can exert over any purer impulse.) A great cloud of dust was kicked skyward as my escort ran off leaving me alone with the leering Philistines. No other companions but stony earth & clods of dirt withered desert plants & birds of prey drifting lazily high against the haze. The walls of the ravine towered up like the mightiest temple imaginable which in a way I suppose it was.

Now I looked at the Philistines and they at me. And they made two mistakes that cost them dear.

The first was in choosing this confined space with its sheer walls and narrow floor. Although the heathens had come in their thousands many of them were clinging to the steep slopes or standing awkwardly one leg higher than the other or leaning backwards so as not to slip. The floor of the ravine was barely thirty paces across so no more than fifteen armed men could face me side by side or perhaps half a dozen grab hold of me at one time.

As I'm sure you know by now half a dozen isn't enough.

They chose this place because they thought they wouldn't have to fight me. That was their first mistake. Their second was laughing about it.

I told you that when I laughed at Hestil the weakling boy I was in error and now the heathens made the same error in laughing at me. Which I suppose shows if anything that there is no tribe of men yet living with an exclusive claim to folly or I suppose immunity from it either.

Which man started it I don't know but it spread fast and in the confined area the echoes bounced and doubled back and melded into such a noise as would make a sane man mad. Not just laughter either but jeers and whistles and unkind comments about my ancestors and mother and father and clan all rolled together. If you've not suffered such scorn yourself— and for your sake I hope you never feel the ill will of thousands of men poured onto you at once from all sides—then I doubt you could imagine the feeling with any accuracy.

But I stayed calm. I let them laugh and hoot and carry on with their boasting and shaking their weapons knowing that eventually it would die out which it did. It withered and choked and rose up again twice or thrice a little weaker each time before settling. And then once again it started but this was the last and it soon paled. The Philistines had had me captured (being too weak to do it themselves) and brought before them (being too cowardly to chase me themselves) and I knew what they were thinking there under the whitewashed desert sky in the deep shadows of the ravine. They were thinking: *Now what?*

I decided to show them what. I lifted my hands overhead and tensed my forearms. The ropes as thick as my wrist and thought to be so strong unraveled and fell away as if woven from water.

Nobody laughed much after that.

How I Became a Judge

Today I woke to the newest chapter in my life. Today I woke up and opened my eyes and nothing changed. I wondered *Have they let the fire go out?* and then I understood. Today I woke up blind.

I have properly learned the name of the Philistine priest who so avidly dogs me: Meneth. He told me this days ago without my asking. And so this morning without thinking I blurted— Meneth I'm blind and heard him breathe sharply through his nose before saying—The ahh least of your worries I should imagine. I wonder how many of your victims you left in the same state hmm?

I ignored his feeble chatter. Even amidst my disorientation an idea had occurred to me—as if with my eyesight gone I could envision other possibilities more clearly. Though to be honest this vague chance was far from clear in my mind at that point.

—Meneth I need to ask you something I said.

—Ask away he answered me—but don't expect much. Criminals get few favors—particularly brutal murderers of innocent people. So it's hard to countenance ahh granting you too much.

He is always saying such things so I ignored this too. It's a kind of game he plays.—Just one thing please I said.—I'm filthy as I think you'll agree.

—Well yes.

—I've been here for I don't know how long exactly. Weeks I think.

—Ahh—quite. Longer in fact but specifics are unimportant. You're looking for a bath I suppose? Hot perfumed water and a dish of fine sand to scrape away the ahh mildew?

—Nothing so grand I assured him.—A wet cloth on my face and behind my neck would do. A slave could do it. And maybe—

I paused. This was the important part so I didn't want to push too much.

—Mm? he prompted.

—If a slave could run a comb through my hair and beard. The itching is something ferocious.

He actually chuckled at this.—You entertain me Samson he said.—What other prisoner has ever had the gall to make such a request? I suppose a pedicure would suit you as well. Some mustard oil for your scalp? A sprig of mint to chew on and a brace of virgins to finger your manhood?

I had plenty to say in answer but didn't wish to displease him: like it or not his goodwill was essential to my getting what I wanted. So I merely muttered—Nothing like that.

—Nothing like that. No I should think not. And so saying he strode off. He hasn't returned yet this morning and whether my ploy will work I know not. But I do have something in mind—faint though it is—and in time we will see if it plays out.

In the meantime let me tell you how I became a judge.

My people the Israelites do not have kings and never have and I for one hope we never do. For a king is but a man after all and will act in his own interest regardless of the interests of his people—if you require any evidence for this my advice is that you unstitch your eyes and look about you. The only king required by my people is the LORD and if they would but remember that in the future then our lives here on earth would be far easier than our history has been up till now.

Following the battle at Jawbone my people groveled before me saying—We know we betrayed you but we were scared and now we see we shouldn't've doubted. Truly the LORD has anointed you our judge so won't you guide us in this difficult time?

I should explain that a judge was no king but something like a guide raised up by the LORD to inspire the people and with no particular authority to make laws or wage wars apart from those he waged himself. However through example he could inspire and such leadership had proved crucial at times in our history. A judge's position as the LORD's favorite lent him no small authority.

Since the massacre at Jawbone the Philistines were torn between desire for all-out war against us and maintaining an uneasy peace born out of fear which you may recall had been my expectation all along. It was apparent that strong leadership was needed to navigate my people through these precarious waters so when I was approached by envoys from each of the tribes I felt compelled to accept their pleas for assistance.

—It's obvious that Yahweh has chosen you before all men they said.—It was prophesied before your birth and is witnessed by your life as a Nazirite. Just as He chose Jephte and Gedeon before you and Debbora before them.

Flattering as such comparisons were I wasn't entirely convinced.—Those you name were beacons in times of darkness I said.—Me I'm just a village boy—a Nazirite it's true but not a very good one if truth be told for I've touched dead bodies on many occasions and tasted wine more times than I care to admit.

—You belittle yourself. Your deeds are as great as any in history—and greater than any man's who yet lives.

In the end I agreed. After all as they asked me and I asked myself and now I ask you: Who was the better choice?

A judge for the Israelites I was for the next twenty years.

Jawbone

No doubt you're impatient to hear what happened when I was delivered unto the Philistines. It wasn't my intention to hold you in suspense but I got distracted what with awakening blind and conversing with Meneth and becoming a judge. So then. Let me recount everything about that day.

The Philistines lost no time in rushing at me once they saw my broken bonds but little good this did them. Stones leaped from the ground to my hands and were deadly missiles that battered down several—others I felled with my hands alone by which time I had a constant source of their own weapons to use against them. Mainly the short bronze swords of this region but also a few stout iron ones left from the Akkadian expulsion and these served me well in hacking the limbs of my tormenters as well as rending their heads while other weapons I threw like vengeful eagles falcons and hawks. I've already said how the terrain of the ravine suited me better than my attackers and so it did as no more than a dozen men could encircle me and their comrades higher up the canyon walls couldn't rain down spears or stones for fear of injuring their own men. At least ten I saw did fall this way before the order was given to stop. After that I had only to confront the limited number directly before me which I did spinning & dodging rending & crushing pummeling & thrashing. Often I used the hacked limbs or headless body of one man as a weapon against the next and even when a blow thus struck wasn't a mortal one still it's amazing how the fight will go out of a man when he realizes what's just hit him.

And in the midst of all this my eye fell upon something on the ground and my hand hefted it up smooth and hard and bent but fitting my palm like a natural piece of my own arm. And it was an old dusty pocked thing—the jawbone of an ass—but let me say this: It was imbued with the spirit of the LORD for it slew more men that day than all the stones bronze and iron combined.

Seeing it there in my hand I reached out with my thoughts and spoke to it and said: *I have need of your aid.*

It answered *I'm ready to give it.*

I thought: *An unorthodox weapon you are but a part of me you must become and together we will make such a slaughter as the world has never seen from a single man.*

The reply was: *I won't fail you.*

And holding that jawbone in my hand with the teeth still gray and knobby within it I felt the peace and serenity of the LORD descend yet again upon me. And this gladdened me for when I felt this peace I knew that death had come for many that day but it hadn't yet come for me.

What happens when I feel this sensation is that everything

becomes very sluggish all around me. I don't remember if I explained this already. The whole world gets slow except for me who moves at a normal speed through it. And the advantage this gives in a fight is obvious as my enemies hobble and lunge with the stiffness of old women while I dance around them like a pup. Whether this is because they are truly sluggish or I am truly fast or if it's just some trick of perception that allows me to anticipate their movements I can't say. But they all appear as stumbling and indecisive and no more substantial than vapor. This plus the jawbone in my hand left all their fury and boasting and weapons as nothing but empty noise. They were curtains to be knocked aside—they were tinder to toss upon the flames. And so I did and watched them burn.

By sunset I had slain a thousand men and left the rest to flee.

Bodies choked the floor of the ravine. I would say their blood stained the earth red but I would be lying because I couldn't see the earth. It was covered with bodies. Corpses were stacked two or three deep and in some places great mounds were piled against the canyon walls. For the latter half of the fighting none of the warriors had stood on the ground—they'd stood on the heads legs and stomachs of their dead brothers and this made for some treacherous footing. More than one of my assailants slipped on the smear of a fallen comrade's opened guts and fell upon a stray weapon before even having the chance to trouble me. And in such small ways does the LORD lend assistance to those who do His work and make His favor known to those who have the wit and eyes to see.

When the fighting was done I climbed out of the ravine. The sun was a low bright circle over the horizon red like a wound in the sky. I was alone for my enemies had run off and my own people had abandoned me. Coated in blood I was—

the blood of others—and dust: my beard was so white with it that I looked like an old man. My mouth was dry as a brick. I hadn't eaten since dawn nor drunk a drop of water and it will be remembered that my day had been eventful.

Still I was satisfied with my work for had I not slaughtered the unbelievers? Killed and killed and killed and isn't that what the LORD wants? Endless blood and death yea until the righteous are brought to victory.

I turned my gaze heavenward and called towards the sky:— With this jawbone of an ass I have massacred a thousand of Your enemies! And then I hurled that bone into the air. High up it flew spinning like a child's toy and at its zenith it seemed to hang against the twilight as if pinned. Then it dropped of course as all earthly things must do: it returned to the dust from whence it came and landed with a soft *pffft* kicking up a cloud.

On my knees now I prayed to the LORD:—You have given me a great victory and I'm grateful for it. You've delivered me from my enemies and that's all any man could ask for. But I said and here I paused.

The red sun slipped behind the hills as I watched.

—But I said—LORD I have a great thirst and even now feel weakness tugging me down like a pack of animals. I fear that if I don't have water soon I will collapse and then perhaps the un-circumcised heathen whom I've lately defeated will slink back and take me in my stupor. Death I fear not but dishonor to Your name shames me.

I paused and wondered what else to say. Around me crickets began chatting with one another in the young night. I decided on the direct approach.—Please Lord send some water and soon. A little rain. A passing stranger. Anything.

And what greeted my ear in response to this? The sound of a fountain. A burbling splash as made only when water shoots some distance into the air before toppling back to earth. Truly my ears deceived me. How could such a thing come to pass?

Stupid question you're thinking and you're right.

The sound came from off to my left some little distance. I stood. Standing up was like trying to lift something very heavy and that thing was me. Every step was an argument but every step brought the sound of rushing water a little closer and with this the effort to move diminished slightly until I got to the source of the sound and my astonishment was such that my exhaustion fled as completely as any terrified Philistine.

There sticking out of the ground was the jawbone where I had flung it. It had come down to bury itself in a spot of loose sand with a bit of its joint end sticking out and also several of the big molars in back. Not all of them of course: the life of an ass is a hard one and some of these teeth had fallen away. And from one of these cavities there sprayed forth a jet of water as thick as my little finger and as pure as a baby's dreams. It spewed into the air to knee height before falling back and had already formed a small pool in the wet sand that was steadily growing. By morning I knew the pool would have overflowed its banks and tipped in a thin cascade over the edge of the ravine and from there collected into a river that would run all the way to the sea washing before it the mounds of dead bodies.

And so it happened. It took time and I was long since gone but it happened. The spring is still there at the bottom of the pool and the waterfall drops over the cliff to form a river. You can go there for yourself and see if you want. The place is called Ramathlechi by the local people which means the lifting up of the jawbone. Anyone can show you. The spring is just called the spring.

I stayed the night drinking often to recover my strength. In the morning I rose and walked south to the villages of my people and some time after that I was declared a judge.

My Time As a Judge

Probably the word judge is misleading as it makes you think all my time was spent in mediation over property disputes or assigning blame for injuries and so on. And while it's true that this took more of my time than I liked—as you shall see—so too did I have other duties. Leading small raiding parties against Philistine warehouses for example. Or ensuring that my people had adequate reserves set aside against famine. And most of all: exhorting them to remember to worship the LORD and not some deaf heathen deity or none at all. Believe me this proved a full-time occupation and not an especially rewarding one.

Although I did more than mediate disputes nonetheless I did so at times and mightily stupid were most of these arguments too. Endless haggling over land boundaries and inheritances and wedding gifts and so forth. So-and-so stole my goat and slaughtered it. No sir—steal it I did not but one morning finding a strange goat on my land I butchered it is this a crime sir? Did you know it was your neighbor's goat? No sir I did not. That's a lie—he saw it had a cropped ear and all mine have such. Is this true? Sir how can I know all of the habits of my neighbors? So then you knew it wasn't one of your animals.

Well yes that's true I suppose but. Now you listen to me: You'll pay your neighbor one goat back to repay his you killed and a second kid too for his trouble in being here today instead of in the field where he belongs and a third kid as payment for your greed. Sir I must protest at this unfairness. Protest all you like my decision stands and the next time one of your animals wanders onto your neighbor's land and he returns it you may thank me for teaching him that property found and kept is no different from property stolen. Now go.

And so they left. The one smug the other sulking and the both fools to my mind for not being able to work this out between themselves. But no sooner were two fools gone than two more appeared in their place.

This man has dishonored me by promising his son to my daughter and then reneging on the agreement! And the reason for this? Sir—my son upon seeing his daughter changed his mind for her manner was rough and not to his liking. Such slander sir do you hear? I'm not deaf and can hear well enough—you there what was your son's objection? Sir it's like this: My boy saw the girl a few times and she pleased him well enough but then he ventured to her farm unannounced one day and saw her treating with the young children most roughly and speaking in a coarse uncultured manner and upon seeing this my son changed his mind. I see and what arrangements had been made? Gifts have been exchanged with certain household items from the girl's family being sent to us. Have they been returned? Yes they have. And your gifts to them? No sign of their return have we seen. Nor shall you dog! Be quiet—I'm the judge here. Apologies sir but really this insult is most intolerable—first he slanders my daughter then shames the family by returning the dowry then insults us further by demanding his gifts. Surely sir you can see the injustice of this? What I see is a young man who changed his mind and one honorable father who returned the offerings and one grasping father lacking all honor who clings like a buzzard clutching at some bit of carrion in its claws. Why I—Attend me: You will return this family's gifts today and if tomorrow I hear that you haven't done so you'll then be required to pay back twice the amount and I will be there myself to collect in person is that clear then?

The one smug the other sulking and both fools.

I must mention one particular dispute brought before me in maybe my tenth year as a judge. A woman had given birth to an infant and then she and her husband divorced but both wanted the child. Precedent sided with the father as the infant was a boy but natural law of a sort compelled the suckling to remain with its mother. Truly it was a case that left me tugging my beard in confusion—the more so because any attempt at compromise was swiftly dismembered by these two who so despised each other I wondered how they had managed to stay civil long enough to disrobe and beget the offspring.

They had each brought their families to plead their side as if there wasn't enough noise already. This was in a village far to the south where the people were strangers to me and even some of their customs felt foreign.

All morning the woman stood before me talking in a low monotone at the ground between her feet. An orange scarf across her hair. She declared the man was a layabout a ruffian a loafer a slave driver no-hoper good-for-nothing ignorant bullying fool and cruel besides. She was only getting started. The man never worked. Had been caught stealing one neighbor's grapes another neighbor's hens the third neighbor's tools and so on. Despite this his wine was sour the hens all died and the tools broke. He borrowed money from the wife's father and gambled it and lost. He coveted neighboring wives and took them when he could and then returned home to beat his own. And so on and it was still morning yet.

In the afternoon was the husband's turn. He smiled at me and promised to speak man-to-man. He was sure I would understand. To put it plainly he said his wife was a whore. This he hadn't known when he married her but he knew it now and was tormented by the idea of his son growing up among such people. His wife neglected to clean the infant or cook for him her husband: she was too busy making eyes at every man in the village and whoever else passed through. In fact—and here he lowered his voice. In fact he suspected his wife didn't even limit her associations only to men. If I knew what he meant. If he could be so bold. He didn't wish to shock me but there it was.

Well then. By the end of this day I was sick of them both. They'd each convinced me that the other was a wretch and unfit to bring up a chicken much less a child. So I called them before me and they stood side by side: him upright and smiling and her with her head down. The infant lay napping quietly on the ground between us. And I said to the woman—You say you want this child?

—Yes sir as only a mother can oh please sir.

To the man I said—And you?

—Yes he said.—I deserve it more for I shall do a proper job of rearing him.

That I doubted but said nothing. Instead I said just to clarify—Then neither of you will renounce your claim?

—No they said together.

—Very well. I've made my decision.

Behind me my sword leaned against my chair. I hefted it now and stepping forward swiftly swung it in a mighty overhead arc that swept down and cleaved the infant in two. So quick this was that the child made not a sound but simply passed from one sleep into that other from which there is no waking.

The woman swayed and fell while the man bent double to vomit a pile of brackish water at his feet. Some people are content to go through life unprepared for the consequences of their actions and such people fill me with scorn.

Around us both families had gone silent and still except for the occasional wail.

I roused the woman and said to her and her husband:—There. You both wanted the child now you can both have your wish. Take a piece and be gone and think carefully before bringing such nonsense before me again. When you present an insoluble problem you're likely to receive an answer that satisfies no one.

Around me were growing up sounds of weeping and gagging and lamentations—a quiet susurration that rose and fell like the sea. Perhaps you think me harsh but I had a point to make and make it I did. Word of this judgment spread rapidly and for the rest of my career I was never bothered again with another such case.

You mustn't think that this type of business laid sole claim to my days but all in all it occupied a larger portion than I would've liked. There were the other duties already mentioned plus the ordinary daily course of life & women business with the heathens & births and deaths. The occasional retaliation against the Ammonites Canaanites or Philistines. Along with ditches to dig and harvests to gather and droughts to endure.

Sometime after this I went to Gaza.

My Weakness for Harlots

I've already confessed my fondness for women of all sorts. It may be recalled that my eye was taken by the jaunty chin and manner of the girl Huneisha who chose to become a harlot rather than the wife of Samson. Well it must be admitted that Huneisha was not the last such miscalculation I ever made. In fact it was one such that landed me in my current dire predicament: head shorn & eyes impotent arms chained & muscles slack. But it's not time to speak of Dalila yet. Her time is coming oh yes it is don't you worry. But before her there is one last episode to tell.

Speaking of my current predicament: in my sightless eternal night the viper Meneth delights in whispering in my ear.—Ho there Samson! he hissed this morning like a very serpent. I would say like the serpent in the Garden but where I am now is no Eden by far.

—Ho mighty one! he murmured with heavy irony. (For irony I have learned is his preferred form of expression.)—Have you availed yourself of this opportunity to ahh reflect on your sins and beg forgiveness?

—I have no sins I said—and nothing that needs forgiving.

The breath out his nose came so sharp it whistled.—Murder on a large scale usually qualifies he said.—Pillage and destruction and the encouragement of others to do the same. Rape of untold numbers of women—

—I've taken no woman against her will. Well maybe one but that was an accident.

—untold numbers as I say carried out by the armies of bandits swarming the countryside and fighting in your name. Farms eradicated. Olive groves burnt fishing nets shredded livestock butchered villages annihilated. You've done such things and your followers much more.

I said nothing but doubtless my teeth were grinding loud enough for him to hear. If only I were a little stronger I would snap these chains as quickly as I would snap this wretch's neck for spilling such venom in my ear. If only.

But remembering my plan—vague though it is—I asked him—Have you given thought to my request?

This gave him pause.—You're speaking of your ahh bath I presume?

—Yes. And comb I added quietly. For Meneth didn't know this but it's the combing part that concerns me the most.

The priest's voice grew calm and icy: a sure sign that he was in a rage. (For when he is angry the irony drops away and the poison shows.)—Believe me your unkempt state will very soon be the ahh least of your problems. Concerns of a more immediate nature are rather more pressing I should think.

—Threats don't scare me I told him.

—Perhaps not. But your actions certainly scare me. Have done for years in fact—terrified me just to think upon. Happily however this state of affairs shall soon change. With you safely dead and news of that event spreading to every corner of this wretched land—then shall peace return.

—Peace I sneered.—What peace can there now be with so much death on both sides?

—And whose fault is that? he sneered right back.—Anyway Samson don't make the mistake of thinking the whole world is as mad as you are. Rational people will lunge at the opportunity for peace once it presents itself. It merely requires the elimination of zealots such as yourself to allow that to occur.

Zealots! There was nothing to say to that. I trust it's obvious to all by now that the LORD has a plan and I am but His instrument to use as He sees fit. If there's anyone still not understanding that—I can't help them.

To take my mind off Meneth's vitriol let me speak of the harlot in Gaza. Gaza was at that time quite a large city and an important one to the Philistines. It's a port city as I'm sure you know—the Philistines being originally sea people who came to Canaan and settled there thus causing strife untold through their unjust usurpation of our land. (Now I've heard it said by vindictive and shortsighted individuals that because Abram later Abraham forefather of the Israelites was himself a migrant to Canaan he was thus no different in kind from the Philistines. And if there's any amongst you who wish to stand before me and say this then by all means do so and I will happily clutch your throat and punch a thumb through your windpipe chains or no chains so that you'll never have the chance to say such an ignorant thing again.)

You may be surprised that I was abroad in the land of the Philistines and could safely journey through Gaza and her surrounding territories—but I had a reputation as a man better left alone and the Gazans had no wish to see their city flattened unto dust in some misguided attempt to slay me. Besides which: the battle at Jawbone had been twenty years before and was an aberration anyway. The war between our peoples was not one of open battles and armies in the field and honorable victory through swift clean slaughter. This is important to understand. It was an affair of mutual suspicion frequent skirmishes and ambush. There was much grasping for political power and frequent bodies dumped into ravines at night. Spies & double agents politicians & other whores. A time of knives in the back and poisoned wine not trumpets blowing down the walls. So an Israelite could go to Gaza and do business if he had business to do and if he avoided trouble then it would most likely avoid him. Best of all if he had money in his pocket it would be welcomed as eagerly as that of any heathen Philistine.

In Gaza I had both business and money which brings me to the harlot. I've always had a weakness for a well-sculpted ankle—this is no secret—and finely turned calf. High arches in the feet don't hurt either. I'm sure this woman had a name a smile and a history but I've misplaced them somewhere. Her ankles though I will never forget. I saw her in the morning on my way to the marketplace as she stood in a doorway in a gray shift down to her feet. In the afternoon as I was seeking a place to nap I saw her in the same doorway in a pink shift to her calves. That evening the shift was red and failed to reach her knees. I got the idea.

In her room she named a figure and I said—All right but I'm staying till morning. She looked a little scared but didn't argue so I pushed her down on her back and went in.

After some time she said—Are you done? and I said—Almost.

Then I went to sleep and woke up later: it was still dark so I went in again and dozed off as it was getting light. Gaza grows noisy early and I didn't get much rest but she looked like she'd had none at all. Before gathering my things to go I went in one more time but it was done in a rush as is often the case in the morning.

She asked for more money. They always do. I said—We had an agreement.

Instead of arguing like I expected she said—If I tell you something that saves your life will you give me money?

She looked terrible in the light of day: hair matted & cheeks sunk teeth missing & eyes that looked like they'd seen unfortunate things. I wanted to tell her to give up her life of sin and transgression before it was too late but considering my recent activities maybe this wasn't the right moment to suggest it. So I said—If what you say is worth it I might.

She dragged some hair away from her eyes and tucked it behind her ear. Long crinkly strands. I always liked that kind of hair and wondered if I should go in her again when she said— They're waiting for you outside the city gates.

—Who?

—City guards. Not all of them she added in a hurry.—Just a few. Youngsters mainly. Plus some hooligans and troublemakers out to make a name for themselves by killing you.

I thought about that before saying—Maybe I should go to your temple and murder your priests as a warning. Then knock the whole thing down. Big as it is I could still do it you know.

(What a sting is in these words now. That temple I spoke of is the one which today holds me prisoner.)

—I know you could she said—but please don't. It's not their idea nor the city councilors either.

—No?

—No. Really.

I stood awhile stumped. In my younger impetuous days I'd've just killed everybody and been done with it and a part of me still favored that approach. But another part wanted to do something calmer and less bloody and who can say why these urges overtake a man from time to time. Maybe in my case it had something to do with this tired sinner with the nice ankles and haunted eyes.

—Outside the gate you say. How many?

—Not many. Two hundred at most maybe less.

In the past I had fought more but this was no ravine. Gaza sat on flat open terrain by the sea and outside the gates two hundred men with the right weapons could conceivably injure even me. Or worse. Unlikely maybe but not impossible. Especially if they were fueled by some misguided notion of vengeance and honor and for my part I felt no more than the desire to leave unscathed.

I asked the harlot—What exactly do they plan?

She sat upon the floor and poured herself a mug of wine.— The rumors are contradictory she said.—Most people agree that they won't seek you within the city walls.

—That's smart of them I said.

—Once you pass through the gates they'll attack. Some say the longer you wait the more their strength will grow. Others say their numbers will dwindle if nothing happens soon.

I sat beside her and reached for the jug. Nazirite or no I needed something to help me ponder. The harlot flinched but passed me a goblet and then as if remembering her duty placed her hand on my knee.—So she said—is such knowledge worth a few coins?

I handed her my purse heavy from the previous day's business.—Take it I said.—You'll need all of it and more if they decide it was you who warned me.

Her face grew hard.—They can't prove anything.

Oh? I thought but said nothing. If the Philistines are such that they require proof before passing judgment on a friendless whore then they are different indeed from most people of my acquaintance.

That afternoon I stayed with her and thought on into the evening. I grew hungry but didn't let the wench go for food lest she stop and talk to somebody. Likewise when a sharp rapping sounded at the door I placed my hand over her mouth and wouldn't let her answer. Later she started to weep from hunger so she said but I shook her a little and she stopped and then I went in her one more time. Afterwards she sat in the gloom rattling the coins I had given her like they were holy icons.

At midnight I left. The streets were dark and quiet with not a lantern glowing but whether this was due to the normal rhythms of the city or to a sense of anxiety and caution I couldn't say. I made my way through dusty lanes lit by the magnificence of stars overhead with only the muttering of animals in their pens for company. Then I came to the city gates and stopped. They were enormous slabs of oak as tall as three men and just as broad. Each was supported on a mighty pillar of granite. They'd been shut for the night and a huge bar of iron-bound oak had been slid into place held tight by a set of huge brackets sunk into the wood. Torches burned along the top. Those torches didn't throw much light but they would throw enough to show me heaving open the bar and trying to slip through the door to the other side. Anyone waiting would have a clear view and even I would be hard-pressed to shrug off fifty or sixty spears hitting home all at once. So my first plan which was to slip away in the dark and be well gone by sunup—killing only those who blocked my path—was swiftly undermined. My second plan was as yet not entirely clear in my mind.

A pair of guards slept in a circle of lanternlight just beside the gate. It wouldn't do to have them sound an alarm so I strangled them where they drowsed and added their weapons to my belt.

From the other side of the gate I heard a voice and stood unmoving until another voice halloed back. I wiped my forehead: the night was sticky and warm despite the breeze blowing across the city from the harbor far behind me. I slipped back into the shadows and wondered what to do. The night wasn't standing still and I didn't want sunrise to find me back with the harlot. But just then a sense of calm fell upon me and I had an idea to try one last maneuver to avoid a confrontation.

The granite pillars that held the gate were as wide as a tall man—meaning I could stretch my arms and wrap my hands around each corner. Fortunately these posts were square-cut not round and better still the ragged and unpolished stone afforded me a sturdy grip. It's true that the column was unspeakably massive but its weight was as nothing to He who created the earth sky sun and all else and I'm referring here to the LORD.

As best I could I cleared my head of stray thoughts and addressed the pillars: *I'm going to tear you out of the ground and carry you away.*

After a long pause the pillars asked *And why would you do that?* And they sounded genuine in their confusion.

To prevent the city's being destroyed I told them. *So that the Philistines will watch me leave without attacking for if they attack me here I will have no choice but to level the gate & the walls the shrines & every last structure in Gaza.*

To this the gates said nothing but their silence was answer enough.

Bending my back into the first pillar and pushing it with all my effort I rent it from the earth with a low tearing sound that I felt in my spine rather than hearing with my ears. Then I relaxed and let the pillar settle and then pulled it towards me and the rest of it tore loose from the ground.

The same then with the other pillar. The oak doors were warped and twisted all out of true now and groaned as dolefully as any man but hadn't broken. The torches along the top had pitched over and fallen to earth where they smoldered and hissed.

Another moment I waited to catch my breath and listen to my heart knocking as it seemed into my head. I was accustomed to a great deal of fast action and strong effort—fighting men & catching foxes taming animals & going in women—but this slow pushing and pulling in stealth was something new. At length my heart settled into a steady rhythm and then I could listen to whatever was happening on the other side of the gate. Which was: nothing. The silence on that side was absolute.

So I took a breath and heaved my shoulders and pulled that gate and those stone slabs onto my back. Once I had steadied myself—the weight was extraordinary but tolerable—I made my way towards the hills overlooking the city from some distance inland.

And if you asked me—What was your purpose in so doing? I'd've had difficulty in giving a proper answer. My first thought was simply to shield myself from the weapons of my foes and using the city gates seemed the likeliest means of this. But only a few steps from Gaza's walls—even as the gates creaked alarmingly and my wrists ached from the effort and great clods of earth broke from the foundations to clump onto the ground amidst heaps of stone and earthworms and many-legged crawling things that scuttled away under cover of darkness—as I say when I had gone only a few steps I realized that inadvertently I had exposed myself to mine enemies for truly they had ringed the city on all sides. But no sooner did I realize this than I saw too that it didn't matter. For the men who were waiting to slay me had been wonderstruck by my feat of strength. Even poorly lit as they were by torches campfires and the occasional smoky taper I could see their terror and awe writ plain on their faces and in the manner in which they held themselves. Like words of fire in the nighttime sky. Much muttering and cursing there was passing all round me as if I was near the ocean and hearing the water lap up against the shore or perhaps beside a river as the current tumbles swiftly by. But it was neither ocean nor current merely the futile imprecations of the heathen as they choked out their blasphemous prayers to their unloving idols who of course heard them not because they lacked the truth presence and holiness of the LORD.

So then. I would like to say I slaughtered them all then and there but I did not. Neither throat was hacked nor backbone crushed though I would have reason to regret that oversight later. O yes. It might've gone easier for me if I had acted without mercy at that moment but it wasn't meant to be.

Instead I just set those oaken gates and granite pillars on the hilltop overlooking Gaza. For all I know they're still there. And then as I had no further interest in the city I walked away. My enemies—having no interest in dying—let me.

Something to Consider

Now we reach that part of my story which is perhaps of greatest interest to you. And maybe you should pause here a moment and reflect as to why this is so.

My Weakness for Harlots—II

Dalila was not a tall woman but a tremendously vital one. I've always been drawn to the quickness of slight women who flit like birds from one perch to another and such was she. Though small she was well formed with hard muscles in her calves and a slim waist and a deep line running down the center of her back. Black hair flashing reddish in the sun. Curly it was and it fell past her shoulders and the woman knew much about keeping it oiled and perfumed and garlanded with loops of small white flowers. She possessed also two neat rows of uncommonly white teeth with none missing at all—merely a slight gap between the two in front which always made me want to poke my tongue there—and was one of those women whose natural tendency when looking upon something or someone unknown is to smile. Perhaps I was especially vulnerable to this: much of my life has been spent being looked upon by strangers who were not smiling and so I found this trait of hers attractive.

Besides all this she had other pleasing physical attributes and talents of a womanly nature which I will leave you to imagine as I've no doubt you're well able to do.

As for her temperament—well it was a changeable thing. During our time together I witnessed many facets of that particular gem. For instance there was Passionate Dalila but also Curious Dalila and then again Sulky Dalila and so forth. As time passed she seemed to try on these tempers one after another as a different woman might change robes. But which of these moods was the closest to her true nature—or whether they all were or indeed if each masked equally the true contours of her soul—I can't answer even now.

The valley of Sorec was where she dwelt with her father: a man who did business for some of the prominent Philistine families there. For Dalila herself was a Philistine but I had no notion to let that fact interfere with her attractiveness. Nor did I have any idea of the true prominence of the families her father dealt with.

The marketplace was where I first looked upon her. I said to myself *Now this is a rare woman.* And I was right. And I thought also *Here is the last woman I shall ever lie with for after her my days and nights of wandering are done.*

Right again I was when I thought that. If only I had known.

Dalila

It's funny how things go. Just yesterday I was thinking on Dalila and this morning the priest Meneth wakes me to my now perpetual darkness and whispers in my ear—The people are singing ahh hymns to your slut.

—I have no slut I answer. Still sleepy I am and unmindful of the wanton cruelty of jailers.

He says—It's the slut Dalila to which I refer. Or do you forget so soon?

I don't answer.

—The people recite poems in her honor he says—and offer prayers for her long life. Songs are sung extolling her glory. Craftsmen carve her likeness to sell and women name newborn girls for her. And you know why?

I turn my thoughts to the LORD and say nothing. LORD I think deliver me from this place. Grant me the strength to kill my enemies for my enemies are Yours and together we shall leave them broken on the plain their wives weeping and their bastard children fatherless.

And thinking thus I feel a little calmer.

Probably you're wondering why I don't turn my thoughts to the chains that bind me as I have spoken in the past to other dumb things. Why don't I tell the manacles that it's time to release me just as the gates of Gaza gave way or the jawbone slew my enemies? The answer is that I've tried and nothing happens. Every day of my confinement I've commanded the chains *You shall break now!* and the manacles *Time for you to shatter!* But to all my urgings & entreaties threats & demands there is only silence. The silence of the truly dumb—or truly dead. Why this is I can't say. Whether it's a weakness due to my shorn and helpless state or whether it's some quality of the iron itself.

Meneth interrupts my thoughts: his words are like a tick in my groin.—They do all this he says—because she has delivered you to us. What ten thousand armed men couldn't accomplish through force one woman has done with the power of her rump. In the villages they're laughing that the mighty Samson was bested by a woman whose chin barely reaches his stomach. By a slut who's lain with more men than a bitch has with dogs.

It's true enough that Dalila brought me to this pass so deny it I don't. As for the rest I can't say. Meneth goes on like this for a time—I've become convinced that talking is his only talent—before growing bored. He shuffles away with a final sigh that's long and heavy as if he has seen much grief that he chooses not to speak aloud. I feel ready to scream and weep. I empty my mind of thought and bellow wordlessly at the chains: *Like twigs you'll shatter and fall away! You have no power and are as shadows upon my flesh!*

In response there is only silence. I am left alone with the dark and my memories.

A Parable

This is a story that Manue my father told me when I was older than a boy but not yet a man. He swore it was true but I don't know.

A traveler was passing beneath a cliff one day when he saw a strikingly shaped boulder jutting out high overhead. The traveler was so taken by the stone that he stopped his camel and gazed wonderstruck. As he watched the sun dipped behind a cloud and the stone's appearance changed. First it looked like a rat then it looked like a fist then again a child's face. Rain began to fall and the stone changed yet again into a breast this time. At sunset the light shone flat against it and its color altered from gray to yellow to pink. The traveler grew excited. He convinced himself that he had discovered an enchanted stone. In moonlight the boulder took on another cast altogether and dawn brought with it dramatic shadows that seemed to spell words. Through all of this the traveler stood or sat or reclined but always gazing upwards and marveling as one change followed the next even as his neck grew sore and his feet numbed. So taken was he that he forgot about his travels his family and his business and moreover paid no notice to the sliding pebbles that trickled beneath the boulder's weight until the stone tipped out of the cliff face and plummeted earthward to crush him. In the final moments of his life the traveler felt only startlement that this thing he had harbored such noble feelings for should prove the agent of his undoing.

Then he died.

I will let you make of that story what you will.

Passionate Dalila or The Trap Is Set

Dalila's father was often busy and her mother was one of those dull colorless women who make no impression. History is full of them. Dalila being the eldest child it was not difficult to arrange a meeting between us in private. This was after I saw her for the first time in the marketplace buying a set of copper drinking vessels. Amidst all the drab and dusty traders her brilliant scarlet robes yellow tunic and purple trousers fluttered like a bee-eater among crows.

I have noticed often in the course of my life that it is the smallest of women who have the largest spirits. Whether this is simply a trick of the eye I can't say but seldom have I encountered a short slightly built woman who wasn't inordinately energetic and vivacious. As if to compensate for their physical frailty they rely instead on laughter and an abundance of liveliness. They remind me at times of sparrows flitting through the trees warbling as they go. Such a one was Dalila who laughed and chattered among the merchants and generally brought uncommon joy to an otherwise everyday scene.

As if led by a tether I followed her from the market down a series of lanes to a small shed. There I had my first chance to speak to her alone and mentioned her attractive qualities as well as the fact that her being a Philistine was no concern of mine. She listened without speaking and then surprised me by lying back on a thick bale of raw wool and hiking up her tunic and letting me go in. It was so sudden and unexpected that I was done nearly before I got properly started and only then did I notice that in my eagerness I had bloodied her nose without intent.

—Sorry I said.

She cast about for a handful of wool to staunch the bleeding.—It's all right she said—don't worry. But she seemed stunned and I did worry a little. She held the stinking fur to her nose and tipped her head back and worked up a smile.—You get quite . . . beside yourself.

—It's not always so but I like you I admitted.—You seem to know what I want.

Her eyebrows lifted.—Is that so unusual? she asked.

I tried to explain.—Doing that with you was like—when the LORD comes to me.

She watched me for a long time and her smile edged away.—Uh huh she said without really understanding. What I meant was that I felt the same light-headedness coursing through me like a painless flame—the rest of the world slowing down and me moving through it quickly and then on her going in. But this was all too complicated to explain.

If I had stopped to consider I might have found it strange that this woman was so eager to lie with me. But then again maybe not. For she wasn't the first such: as I have indicated before there was never a shortage of women who found me comely. Moreover I was well aware that she was a Philistine living in Philistine lands and no one needs reminding about the dissolute habits and sinful ways of the unbelievers.

We were in a storage shed at the edge of her father's property that he used for the goods he traded. Like my own father he did a bit of this and that but unlike Manue avoided dabbling in things agricultural preferring to trade solely for what the household required. As a result there was no shortage of servants and boys and animal tenders underfoot and I half expected to be interrupted at any moment by someone come to the shed to gather merchandise or make a delivery or count inventory. But over the many weeks that Dalila and I met there this never happened. Every day we lay together except sometimes when she was unclean (sometimes even then) and I went in twice or thrice each day but in all that time nobody ever approached the shed besides us. Looking back now it's all quite obvious but at the time I was blinded by lust. Nor am I too proud to admit this. You might think me a fool to be so distracted but let me tell you the LORD has gifted each of us with unique talents and the talent that Dalila had was carried in her cunt. I don't apologize for this bluntness and if it offends you all I can say is that I'm a man given to speaking plainly in all things so as to avoid misunderstanding. For I have lain with many women and they are all different. Some lie like logs while you heave against them and leave you wondering. Others stare back with fear or pain which has an appeal of its own but isn't enough to sustain desire for any length of time. Still others act as if Judgment Day has already arrived and they've yet to decide whether you're taking them to Heaven or Hell. Some women offer endless advice and imprecations and pleas and assurances and so manage to distract you from your own pleasure. And then there are many who make a great pretense of excitement with their sounds & rolling about flapping arms & legs hurled in all directions which simply makes everything false and unsatisfying.

Dalila did none of this. Indeed a kind of sympathy grew between our bodies. She understood what I wanted and how and when. Besides this there was the physical aspect which I must mention despite its indelicate nature. Being a large man makes me large in all respects and many women have cried out in pain when they discovered just how large. Yet Dalila despite her short stature took me in easily and even as her ankles squeezed my ribs urged me to move with more vigor. And you must believe me when I say I had not often heard those words and needed little encouragement.

Most of all I was taken by the eagerness of her appetite. Later I would think of her at this time as Passionate Dalila. Some women have more desire than others but never had I met one who had as much as I. Of course in the end I discovered that much of this was dissembling and mimicry but I flatter myself that a portion at least was genuine. Exactly how much was real and how much falsely arranged I leave you to decide.

After that first time I never bloodied her again except of course when she was unclean and that was no fault of mine.

This went on for quite a while.

What I Didn't Know Then

We didn't marry. This perhaps disturbs you but my experience with marriage wasn't a happy one so when she brought up the matter I dismissed it. She didn't seem overly upset but I could tell it crossed her thoughts from time to time. As weeks passed I began to hear rumors that we had in fact been wed. Whether this was Dalila's doing or not I couldn't say but I have my suspicions. At that time I wondered if it was a ruse by some quick-thinking Philistine to lull my people into believing all was well between our nations—and so gain some sort of advantage. But I could see no gain to be had from this so I shrugged it off. In any case I never held these rumors against Dalila as a woman's reputation is a fragile thing. But the result of her conniving is that the truth of the matter was muddied and remains so to this day.

I stayed in that valley for some months and although it was a Philistine area I experienced no trouble. It seemed to me that—whatever grievances they imagined they'd had in the past—they decided to lay them to rest and I couldn't have said whether this was due to their previous defeats at my hands or to some previously undiscovered respect for my status as judge. But if I had to guess I wouldn't guess the latter.

While in the valley I lived with an Israelite family in the poor quarter but I paid them little attention. In fact I paid little attention at all to the needs of my people although their situation at this time was dire indeed. This fact doesn't reflect well on me but it's the truth which is why I'm telling it. For notwithstanding the rise in my personal fortunes the situation in the world at large remained as bleak as ever. The Philistines and Canaanites having learned that they couldn't subdue my tribe through force had turned instead to the plow and ax and seized much territory which had either lain unclaimed or else been the periphery of Israelite lands. Philistine fields spread inland like mold and their villages expanded into towns and towns into cities. Of course they gave preferential treatment to their own people in business. And there were many instances of violence with families being slain in their sleep and whole villages torched and lands stolen. If I could have resisted I would've but even I couldn't be in all places at once and our enemies understood this. Then the Ammonites in the desert got into the act—raiding our villages from their nomad camps to the east as we were pressed by the Philistines to the west.

And so my people got squeezed as if between two momentous unholy hands.

And I cared not. For I had Dalila's muscular calves and tiny waist and magical loins to distract me and distract me they did.

But what I didn't know was this. Dalila was even at this time in the service of the Philistine princes who'd selected her to be my seductress. These princes—for so they call themselves though really they are no more royal than I but are simply the male heirs of certain wealthy families who managed to claw their way to prominence and then fight off their challengers— these so-called princes had decided to do with low cunning what they couldn't achieve with honest murder. They hatched a plot in which to snare me and cast about for the perfect bait. And found it in Dalila. Found her willing and even—as I said before—eager. And I think I know why. For I've observed that although many women tolerate the circumscribed course of life allowed to them others do not. Some women cast about seeking challenges just as their brothers do but since so many spheres of ordinary human endeavor are closed to them— trade & finance warfare & sport exploration & adventure priesthood & scholarship—they are left to exploit that one sphere of intercourse which is open unto them. And if you think I use that word *intercourse* casually you're wrong. So then. Dalila being one of those women had long pondered my reputation with a lust—not merely sexual but also of the type that grasps for power & fame glory & reputation of the sort that lingers long after death—and she must have rejoiced when given the opportunity to act upon her desire.

—It won't be easy these so-called princes told her. (Or so I imagine it in my mind.)

—It matters not she answered with a feisty toss of her curly head. (Shiny with oil that hair would've been or with a ring of flowers tucked among her brows.)

—You'll have to lie with him they warned.—Probably more than once.

—That is nothing to me she shrugged.

The princes exchanged hungry looks. (Or so I imagine.)—Do you understand what is required? You must learn the secret of his power so we can overwhelm him. He is a curse on us and his strength comes from no natural source that much is sure.

—That's what intrigues me she said.

The oldest prince had not much hair and fine lines across his forehead and stains dotting his chin like venereal scars. Licking his lips he said—We must also ensure that you've got the proper skills for the task. He's a big man and you'll have to be strong.

—I'm strong enough to lie with any man she said.—Care to see?

And then like a warrior she pushed them back on their fine cushions and hoisted her tunic and fucked them all one after the next.

A Hopeless Lie

The princes didn't expect Dalila to do her whoring for free and the price they agreed to pay her upon my capture was eleven hundred pieces of silver from each of them. Think on that a moment. Eleven hundred from *each*. That's more money than any reasonable man can easily imagine. And Dalila? How many sailors and merchants and farmers would it have taken her to collect even a fraction of that amount?

So I'm not surprised she agreed to it. Many women would've done so and not a few men too. What does surprise me every time I reflect on it is that the princes were so able to perfectly match siren to victim. As if they could look upon my longing and read it like one of our sacred scrolls and then design a woman perfectly matched to the lineaments of my desire. And thus do the sinners of this world conspire to topple those who would do the LORD's righteous works.

For the truth was I had lived a solitary and violent life for many years. Both as warrior and judge I was a figure commanding respect and fear but little fondness. Nor yet love. No—these more tender feelings inhabited a different sphere from that through which I walked. And whether the princes could see this—which is hard to imagine—or if it was Dalila's doing I can't say.

So you can see how vulnerable I was. How dire my weakness. It's said that pride comes before a fall but in my case it wasn't pride alone. Other things were mixed in too: lust and loneliness and some sort of a desire for a quiet place to rest. The Philistines divined all this somehow and used it against me. Not that I blame them. Our peoples were at war after all even if the armies had retreated from the countryside and in war anything is permissible.

Speaking of war: Meneth came to me just now to vomit more poison into my ear. If I were a more reflective man I might wonder what kind of satisfaction it gives him to do this—what kind of charred heart can be warmed by inflicting pain on others. But I'm not such and so I didn't wonder about this thing for long.

He said—I have news.

—I don't want it I told him.

—It's too momentous to miss he said.

—If you won't send a servant to comb me then would you at least scratch my head? It itches.

He was silent for a long space but I could hear the whistling of his breath. At length he spoke calmly:—You seem to think I'm your slave to rub you when you suffer. Or perhaps a wench to suck your cock. Disabuse yourself of these notions forthwith.

I shrugged. All I've wanted for some time now is an idea of how long my hair has grown—for against all expectations these fools don't seem to understand what it signifies. But I will have to devise some other way of learning this. So I said—This news of yours. Is it really news or just idle rumor and gossip?

—What's the difference? He shrugged.—What matters is that there is great rejoicing among the Philistines and Ammonites. A sense of optimism grows within the people. They say peace has come to our troubled land at last.

—Peace? What peace?

He inhaled deeply as if his words were wine on his tongue that he needed to savor.—The peace that will come with your death. For too long you have terrorized my people. You prey on them for your own gain and personal glory.

—What nonsense I spat.

—How many innocent men have you murdered Samson? Consider a moment before answering. Five thousand? Ten? Twenty thousand or more? Things get exaggerated but it's hard to know who's more guilty of that—your victims or your supporters.

I reminded him—I killed no man who didn't deserve it. They were guilty.

—Guilty? Of ahh defending their homes perhaps? Planting crops? Loving their children too much?

—I didn't start this war.

—You've certainly made it worse.

I had to laugh.—And you'd've done differently in my place?

—Perhaps not he admitted.—But I'm not in your place. Nor am I a formidable enough individual to wreak such destruction. Nobody is. But there's something more. Seeing what you've done over all these years has brought many of us to the conclusion that this war is futile. That this endless striving for supremacy must be abandoned and some manner of balance maintained.

—What you mean I sneered—is that having been whipped—by me—like the dogs you are you're unwilling to allow yourselves to be whipped again so now you're preaching peace. I see through you like a window Meneth. It's easy to say fighting is pointless when you've already lost.

—The balance must be maintained he repeated. Then leaned close to whisper in my ear:—And so it shall be—when you are dead.

—With me dead there'll be nothing to prevent your princes from mustering armies and terrorizing my people in return for my alleged crimes against you. That's the only kind of balance you respect.

—You're wrong he said. His voice took on a conciliatory tone as if he was trying to be reasonable.—Look he said—we are all immigrants to these lands. Israelites and Philistines and Ammonites and the rest. The only natives left are the poor Canaanites and they're so beaten down they hardly matter anymore.

Just hearing those words made me sick to my stomach.—
My people have nothing in common with yours I gritted.

—Oh please. Your ancestor Abraham came from the north
just like half the villagers in Canaan. Only he was Abram then
and changed his name once he got here. Look I'm not here to
argue history—

—Oh?

—but to tell you that history has passed you by. Don't you
understand yet? You're a relic from a past that has grown irrelevant. The only path to the future is through renunciation of
violence.

—Let's just see about that.

—Yes he said and he sounded almost sad. But I didn't let his
theatrics fool me for these people are famous for their
duplicity.—Yes indeed we shall see. All the highest families
from every Philistine town and city will be on hand to watch
your execution and all our best military minds as well. And
then we shall celebrate your death with a fete unlike any ever
known on earth. And then you know what we shall do?

—March on my people. Slaughter the men and rape the
women. Enslave the children & salt the fields fire the buildings
& burn the orchards. Erase our very memory.

Tears stung my eyes as I said this. As I saw this.

—How ahh quaint he replied.—But happily how wrong as
well. After the fete and the pyre that will carry off your last
ashy remains—we shall all *go home.*

I said nothing to this obvious lie.

—Home to tend our wives and farms he said.—I shall return to the temple in Hebron where I belong. The Ammonites
will bring their caravans to our villages. Philistine shall not attack Israelite nor shall Israelite attack Philistine. Our villages

will prosper. At first there may be some mutual suspicion as we have little to do with each other but as time passes and our people flourish we shall once again walk side by side. Working together we shall reclaim this bleeding land and in what—a thousand years? Two thousand? At some blurry point in the future all this trouble will be ancient history best forgotten and—listen well—happily consigned to oblivion.

He went away with his lies ringing in my head. Lies of peace and tolerance and brotherhood. And I gnashed my teeth and prayed for the jaws of a rat that I could gnaw through these chains. Then I would show them peace. Show them all the peace of the grave with me standing above them with their blood black on my hands and the hand of none other but the LORD giving me shelter succor and delight.

Curious Dalila or The Trap Is Baited

—Talk to me Dalila urged.

She had a habit of asking things on those afternoons when we lay together like husband and wife although we were not. Those afternoons were often hot and always drowsy with our exertions and the stifling air of the hut in which we concealed ourselves.

—About what? I asked.

—Anything. Where you came from. Tell me about your village.

—Hot I said.—Rocky soil. But still it's home so that counts for much.

Later it was:—What are your parents like?

So I told her.

And then:—Have you ever been married?

—So I have I said.—Are you sure you want that story? It'll take some time and might be more than you bargained for.

Giggling and biting her lip she said—I *think* so—so I went ahead and told her everything about that too. This silenced her for a time as well it might.

Maybe I should've asked her what she thought of Huneisha's actions. And my own. But I never did and now I wonder if that was an oversight on my part.

Then she said—Tell me the source of your strength Samson.

Many wondered about this—that I knew—but none had dared ask so the question took me by surprise. Since childhood it had been impressed upon me by my parents that this secret must never be divulged. So I had held it close to me like some precious thing—like a totem of power or a holy relic hidden beneath a pilgrim's robe. Dalila however seemed intent on prying it loose.

—Your strength. Where does it come from and how—how could you be made weak?

Before long Curious Dalila was asking this constantly. As mentioned earlier I was quite distracted by lust or I would've thought it odd how she returned to this same theme day after day as if preoccupied. Admittedly she mixed in many harmless distracting questions along with this other one (Do you prefer my hair tied up with garlands Samson or hanging loose like this around my breasts so that my nipples show through?) but nonetheless if you thought me as blind then as now I would have no cause to argue.

—Tell me she cooed.

Her interest was only natural or so I assured myself. For she was after all a woman of slight build and so would be curious about the secrets of a powerful man such as I. And as we were intimate so often and in so many ways could her desire for further intimacy not be forgiven?

—Tell me! She giggled. A strange mix of girlishness and earnest entreaty ran through her words. Refusing her at such moments risked bringing an appearance by Petulant Dalila. And if you grow impatient with my dullness in not grasping the true situation I can only ask that you bear with me for some time—as this dullness was to last quite a few weeks and if you are growing tired of it already then you'll be well and truly sick of it before my tale is finished.

Day followed day and nobody happened across us in the shed and still it didn't cross my mind to wonder.

—*Tell* me . . .

Lying beside me as she did her bosoms pressed against my stomach and her hair spilled across my chest and her fingers lingered I will say not where. The smell of her on me and I suppose of me on her. Pleasant indeed were these interludes. But even so: I had few enough secrets that those I did have I carried close to my heart and didn't give up easily no matter who was asking. So I contented myself with playful answers.

I told her—The secret of my strength is the rain.

And Dalila lifted her head up from my belly and blinked at me sleepily and said—The rain?

—The rain that falls I answered. The Lord's gift from Heaven and each time it strikes the earth I grow more powerful.

—I see she said after a time.

—So you'd best hope there's no flood I said.—Else I will become too much for even your mighty thighs to contain.

But I've never been good with jokes and couldn't keep from laughing aloud at her gullibility and her face grew pinched and flustered when she realized I mocked her but besides this she said no more.

Petulant Dalila then returned for a little time.

When next she asked I said—The milk from my mother's teats gives me my power. That is why I must periodically return to her even now to suckle and replenish myself. But this time Playful Dalila was expecting more mockery so only slapped my chin—lightly—and held out her own teat which was barely smaller than any matron's saying—No need to bother your poor mother anymore now that you have this. For a moment I thought she meant she was with child from our coupling but this wasn't so and I admit I was just as glad for it. For although I knew that children were the natural result of our furious exertions our situation was an odd one and becoming a father would've placed shackles of a type on me— necessitating a resettlement in some quieter haven than a Philistine stronghold like Gaza so that the child could be raised among godly people and learn godly ways. I was long since old enough to have settled into my unsettled habits—roaming and judging and lying with whatever woman I fancied—and uncertain whether this ordinary kind of life held any appeal.

Now of course it holds much.

(I've often wondered since that time whether Dalila was taking steps to prevent the begetting of children. I never asked but it seems likely. The heathens have many such methods or so it is said.)

When Dalila next asked after my strength I told her that the sun gave me my power and after that it was my sandals which was why I always wore them when we lay together. (For so I did: I enjoyed the urgency of not waiting to undress fully.) Once I said there was a worm living in my belly. As the weeks passed it became a game for me to think of new and always different sources of strength. This wasn't easy as such mental diversions weren't my usual amusement. But to my surprise I found that I enjoyed the challenge.

Once I said:—You hear those birds flying past? They're the source of my strength. Kill them all and I'll be helpless.

Or again:—Honey is the secret. A ladle of it each morning.

Or yet another time:—Your cunt nourishes me woman. Withhold it from me and I will curl up as weak as any infant.

But this was the day I took it too far and she became Weepy Dalila—weak and trembling and quite unlike the Frolicsome Dalila I had grown used to who always had a ready answer and a quick tongue and flashing smile. Suddenly she was keening like a widow and crying out—Why do you mock me so?

Surprised by this outburst I didn't trust myself to speak.

—Why not tell me the secret of your power and yes of your vulnerability too? If I meant anything to you—anything at all—you'd not hide the truth from me!

This caused me to pause and think. I decided she was probably right. And although I wasn't in love with Dalila—not in the way that love is sometimes spoken of by poets—neither yet did I wish for such scenes as these to become commonplace between us. There is little that can take away the pleasure of lying with a woman quite so fast as that woman's eruption into soggy tears soon afterwards. Besides which I will admit to some tenderness towards her. It's I think impossible for man and woman to lie together as often as we had and not develop some feelings. Whether fondness or animosity is all unknown till it happens: but complete apathy is possible only among insects and lizards not human beings.

So I will admit that it pained me to look upon her weeping. A small aching nugget took root just behind my stomach and it wasn't a sensation I enjoyed.

—Listen I said.—My strength comes from the LORD but as for why He chooses to give it to me I can't say. But I can tell you how I can be bound so that I can't break loose. This secret of my weakness is known to no other. Will that satisfy you?

At this she wiped her eyes and grew attentive.—Tell me.

—My arms I said and held them out before me wrists together.—If my arms are bound together so with seven cords of sinew yet wet then I will become as weak as any man.

—Sinews she said.—Seven sinews. Her eyes glittered—with tears I assumed.

—It's true on my honor I told her.—But they must be fresh and still wet or I will snap them as easily as—Here I pinched one of her curls between my finger and thumb—your hair.

—I see she said. Then wiping her eyes she gave me a brave smile and pulled herself atop me with her teats hanging down and spreading across my belly.—Well it's of no consequence anyway is it?

—I should think not.

—But thank you for telling me she said kissing me lightly on the breastbone.—Thank you for trusting me enough to take me into confidence.

My hands held her rump. Round as melons but smoother and softer. This was all that occupied my thoughts as I said—Speak of it no more.

And so she didn't. That day.

Tender Dalila or The Trap Is Avoided

Two days after this we again met and lay together and on this morning Dalila was—there is no other word for it—insatiable. I've heard it said that certain animals and even some tribes of human beings living in distant lands contain females given to extraordinary sexual appetites and this day did Dalila indeed remind me of some not-altogether-human thing. I don't mean to echo the old tired prejudices of my people and hers which each claim that the other side is deviant and prone to unhealthy fetishes and practices (although that may be true enough from what I've heard). I'm talking about something on an altogether grander scale. Once an itinerant tinker close by Hebron told me that a she-cat can couple with twelve different males between sunrise and midday and then another twelve between midday and dusk and then another twelve between dusk and midnight and so on for three consecutive days. He had seen this with his own eyes or so he said.

On the day I speak of now Dalila carried that cat within her spirit.

First I had her and barely had I finished when she begged for it again. I took her rougher this second time with her bent low like an animal before me for so I especially enjoy it but no sooner had I reclined afterwards to recover my breath than she was clambering upon me her thighs slippery and her bosoms slick with a layer of sweat. Roughly she smeared her loins against my own saying—Surely such a big strong man has more than that at his disposal?

David Maine

—Of course I said but for a time I wasn't entirely certain. However Dalila being a woman of extraordinary gifts soon resurrected my sleeping powers. That third time was I think our longest and laziest coupling yet. Exhausting as well: barely had I finished with her than I dropped off into slumber as if drugged.

Strange dreams awaited me there. Spiders and butterflies and webs and concealment. A wise man might've made head or tail of them but a wise man I am not. At the time they meant little to me and I admit they're just as baffling now.

I woke on my side, which was unusual for I always sleep on my back. That was the first thing. The second thing was that some slight nagging tug pulled at my wrists when I tried to stretch my arms. My eyes opened more fully.

A voice I didn't know said—He's awake!

A man's voice this was.

Then another said—Get ready he may try something.

—What can he try? said the first.—We got him trussed like a pig.

Well this angered me as you can imagine.

—Dalila I said.—Dalila where are you?

—Oh Samson! she cried and I heard the fear in her voice.—Samson! The Philistines have fallen upon us both while we slept and have bound you! We are both doomed unless you can do something to save us. Beg for our lives Samson lest they grow angry and kill us!

Fully awake now I sat up and snapped the ropes behind me like threads. Like threads gone soft with spit. There in the hut were crammed six or seven heavily armed ruffians—Philistines all and hard scarred men—with Dalila cowering among them. It angered me to see her helpless and half naked like that.

144

There was much I didn't know at that moment—but I didn't know that then.

When the men saw my arms free their demeanor changed as well it might. They went from being confident arrogant bullies with weapons to being scared sweaty children with toys. I jumped to my feet and killed them. I don't remember how they died: they aren't worth remembering. Probably I used my hands although maybe I snatched away their weapons and used them to open their throats. Honestly I couldn't say except for the last two who I questioned.

—Who sent you?

—Don't kill us!

—Who sent you?

—Sir we were in the market and a man brought us money we don't know who he was he never said his name—

When I cracked their heads together they folded into each other like old fruit. I wiped my hands dry on their tunics then to Dalila I said:—We aren't safe.

All she said in response was—Indeed.

She looked pale and sick whether from the attack or from the violence of my response I didn't know. I reminded myself that she was only a woman and so unused to such scenes. Taking hold of her elbow I said—It's all right now they can't hurt us.

After a moment she swallowed and said—I'm glad to hear it. But we shall have to be more careful from now on.

Her words *from now on* confused me. I said—What do you mean? We can't continue as we have that's plain. We need to stop.

She looked at me with genuine fright and whispered—Don't say that. We were careless—we fell asleep—they snuck in and tied us. All right. We made a mistake but we know better now. We shall find a new place and be more alert.

The longing in her voice was easy to hear. Like a widow's lament or the unexpected call of a beast against the night. If I'm honest I will admit: I felt it too.

—I don't know I said.—I have a bad feeling about this. I've been here too long and too many people know my habits. They know about our meeting here. Most people will leave me alone but there's always a hothead ready to make trouble.

I hesitated.—Maybe I should just go I said.

—Go where?

—Home.

—Don't say that she said.—Please don't.

And she started to cry.

I didn't know how to answer. I had the strange feeling—strange to me but maybe not so to other men—that I was mixed up in something I couldn't handle. Something bigger and more powerful than myself. I was right of course but didn't know just how right.—Dalila I said but couldn't think what to say next. I asked the LORD for help but He remained silent on this one. It occurred to me that He was a fair bit better at guiding my hand to slay my enemies than guiding my tongue to set my friends at ease.

Dalila turned away. She had partially dressed herself while I was sleeping and I could see her tunic all scuffed and dusty from where it had lain on the ground. Her shoulders were shaking and all around her were corpses draining into the mud floor of the hut. I imagined her walking away from me and not returning. Where would I go? Back to my parents? My village? I didn't want to go alone. Dalila hadn't even left yet and already I felt the absence of her like the presence of something else. Something had happened to me: being with her made me feel like the earth itself—large and solid and unchanging—

while she spun around me hot and bright and small like the
sun. I liked the way this made me feel. I had never felt it before
and didn't want the feeling to be lost.

I said her name again.

She turned to me and her tunic fell open as her eyes met
mine.—Please she said.

May the LORD help me but I agreed.

Sulky Dalila or The Trap Is Reconstructed

After this we met in a different place. It was a barn
close by Dalila's house used not for animals but for storing
grain and supplies. A silo I guess you'd call it. It was larger and
airier than the shed we had gotten used to and this should've
made it pleasanter as well but after our last encounter I found
myself nervous with its high ceiling dark corners and shadowy
nooks. I'm not saying that I didn't enjoy Dalila just as much
because I did. If anything maybe a little more than before as
our couplings were now fueled with a strain of tension previously absent. But I was never completely at peace in that place.

Not that it mattered to any great degree. Dalila soon returned to her previous state of doting and lustfulness and little
encouragement was needed for me to join her. The only problem was that Dalila's feelings had been stung when she learned
of my duplicity in confessing to my supposed weakness.

—You mocked me she said one afternoon as we lay spent.—
You told me a lie and enjoyed the deception.

Well I thought this pretty unfair and told her so.—If I had
told the truth I reminded her—then where would we be now?
Both of us in some Philistine dungeon most likely.

She pouted.—The prison's not been built to hold you she said.

—True enough so most likely they'd just cut my throat.

Still she said—Why don't you trust me?

There was no answer to this other than saying I was reluctant to trust anyone with knowledge that could kill me but I sensed this would be an unwise thing to voice. So I said only— Be glad I didn't trust you for obviously someone was listening and got the idea to try what he heard.

—No one's listening now she murmured.

I was less sure of this than she.

Her fingernails were long and oval. She was the only woman I ever knew who managed to keep them clean not crusted with dirt or grease or bitten off or ragged. When she ran them across my chest it caused my nipples to ache and I wondered if this was something like the feeling that new mothers get when their breasts swell and they yearn to suckle their newborn. It wasn't exactly pleasurable but neither yet did it quite hurt. I said—How do you keep your fingernails so clean?

—Stop trying to change the subject she said.

—It's as if you do nothing all day besides make yourself desirable for me.

Even her laughter managed to be sulky like an unhappy dove.—Would that bother you so much? If I stopped helping my father and did nothing but wait on your pleasure?

I wasn't entirely clear on what exactly her father did or how she helped him but I let it go. I had asked before but the answers tended to vagueness. Not having much experience with vagueness—most people were happy to give me a direct answer when asked for one—I was unsure how to proceed and so had put the question aside.

—Anyway I shall stop asking for your confidence Dalila announced. Her voice dropped low and the hurt in it was plain.—If I'm just a harlot to you a tramp to enjoy and forget about—

—I never said that I said.

—then I should expect nothing more.

I made up my mind.—Okay I said—but look. We need to be on our guard. We can't let what happened before happen again. We might not be so lucky.

Her eyes were enormous and so deeply brown as to be black with brows growing thick above them in little arcs. They almost met in the middle in a little bridge above her nose but not quite.—All right she said and nodded. And smiled just a little bit like she was hopeful of something good. Her eyebrow-arcs lifted as if expecting some great gift.

And then I told her.

More Provocations

Twice a day a slave brings me a bowl of swill and feeds me. Before my sight failed entirely I could catch her eye—for woman she was and so tall and brown as to lend her an uncanny aspect—and give her a nod or weak smile. For we were both prisoners in that place and I'm not ashamed to say I reached out to her in an attempt to give us both some comfort. She smiled back wanly but never spoke when I murmured into her ear as she stood beside me and lifted the spoon to my mouth. Whether this was due to fear of our captors or some other disinclination—maybe she failed to understand my language or maybe her tongue had been cut out—I didn't know. After a time I stopped trying.

This same woman feeds me now—so I believe because of the way her chains rattle and the angle of the spoon as it is lifted to my lips. Also there was a particular wheezing to her breath when she stood near me which is unchanged.

I have my reasons for discussing this servant at such length and will reveal them later.

The swill she feeds me is inevitably cold and greasy and bordering close enough to rancid for me to refuse it as often as not. Sometimes when I do this there follows an improvement in the quality of the food for a time. From this I've concluded that my captors don't wish me to starve to death beforehand but rather have some plan for my execution. And thinking this I remember Meneth's gloating.

Today when the slave comes the priest comes with her so I ask—Were you telling the truth that time?

—I always tell the truth he says glibly.—You refer to ahh what exactly?

—When you said my execution is to be a public event. That all your generals and princes and fine families are coming to watch me die.

—Ahh yes. Count on it.

I think on this for a bit. The plan has set up camp in the remotest corners of my mind but is still tenuous and unclear and I fear to look on it directly lest it fade. So I say—Maybe you'll grant me my wish for a bath before that time.

—Count on it. He chuckles.—And we shall comb out the snags in your beard and dress you in fine robes for after all you must look your best.

The words lift my heart but I struggle not to let it show. Instead I say—Do I really mean so much to your people?

He laughs aloud at that and says—How important you are to

us is irrelevant. What matters is how important you are to your own nation. Once you are safely dead we shall spread the news like a flood and in so doing—as I explained earlier—dampen the grandiose military aspirations that have plagued us for so many generations.

His words needle me I admit.

—You've some nerve to talk of plagues I say.—Was it not my people the Israelites who were held captive by the Egyptians? Who were enslaved for more generations than you claim to have been at war with us? Who were delivered from their captivity by a renegade prophet who called down the plagues of the One True God upon the unbowed heads and firstborn sons of the unbelievers?

—So it is said. By your own kind primarily but even by some others too.

—Well then I say.—The righteousness of our cause cannot be argued.

His voice is like grease spilled upon a bath.—But even assuming it's all true I have a question.

—I'm not interested in your questions I say.—Though I suppose that will do me no good.

—I suppose not he murmurs.—Being as you are blind chained helpless and strung up. Fortunately for your limited intellect my question is a simple one. Supposing all your tales are true—the subjugation captivity and humiliation—the enslavement—the bricks without straw the infant in the basket floating down the river—the magic tricks in front of Pharoah—

—You watch yourself I growl.

—and of course the frogs hail locusts rain of blood entrails smeared upon the lintels and so on. Wonderful stories I grant you. But even supposing every word is true: Why should a single Canaanite have to die for it? And why must any Philistine be forced to compensate for your miserable history? What does it have to do with *us*?

How I wish for a free hand then. Just one would be enough. Or even just my vision that I might spit in his eye and blind him with its venom for such is my fury at his words.

Instead I'm left to quiver—How dare you! Which sounds weak and impotent which of course is what I am.

His reply seems genuinely confused.—How dare I? I dare because it's the obvious question to ask. You were held captive. Then you were led out by Moses—that's pure inspiration. Really. Nothing to complain of there. You may recall it was the Egyptians who held you not the Philistines or Ammonites and when the Red Sea parted and then came crashing back again it was Pharaoh's charioteers who drowned not any of my people. But the next thing we know—historically speaking—you've got an army on the prowl sacking cities razing farms kicking down the walls of Jericho and torching the place. And that's just the start of it. What did the poor Canaanites ever do to you? What crime did the innocents of Hai and Maceda and Lebna and Asor commit that they deserved to be slaughtered? For that matter—why should my people the Philistines suffer today for crimes they never perpetrated against yours?

I admit to barely listening anymore. For one thing he's obviously ignorant and for another he is one of the many who have simply chosen to despise all Israelites and blame them for every one of the world's ills. Sad to say but there are many such. But the main reason for my distraction is his reference to Josue and the mighty battles he presided over so long ago. Regrets are not a thing I'm prone to but I will admit this: I wish I had been present on that day when boulders plummeted from a cloudless sky to crush the infidels—and the sun stood still in the zenith allowing the bloodshed to go on and on without cease. They say there was no day like it before or since and they're right. What it must have been like to be there when city after city of the sinners was burned to ash! Or earlier still at Jericho: when the ram horns blew and the angels' trumpets answered and the walls collapsed into rubble and dust. Whatever heathen survived that calamity didn't survive for long. What a slaughter there must have been when the army razed the city and what joy for a man to stand ankle-deep in blood.

After a time I realize that Meneth's voice has fallen silent. Then he says—Well? and I say—Well what? and he says—Won't you deign to answer me? For all your faults Samson I'm the first to admit that inscrutability isn't one of them.

—Only the One True God can answer your questions I say.—He ordained it all and He's the only one who can make clear His motives.

—You've no better answer than that?

—There *is* no better answer than that I tell him.—But I will add this. You're talking about ancient history. All this worrying about who did what to who and when it's in the past. You can't change the reality here and now Meneth.

He seems to choke as I'm talking.—Ancient history! he gasps at last.—As if you're interested in anything but!

I don't know what he means by this. History has never been any great interest of mine and I say so before adding—It's the events of my lifetime that have shaped me. And in my lifetime we are enemies and our children would be too if we had any. That's what matters.

—And you've learned this I suppose from that deity that you're always nattering on about?

I refuse to be baited. Calmly I tell him—Amongst other sources. My own eyes for example.

He's unsatisfied but who cares? There's little he can do about it besides kill me. I'm not pretending to be heroic for I've no wish to die but I've had plenty of time to consider it lately and if it happens so be it. But my death will not inconvenience the LORD or deviate Him from His plan by so much as the width of a rat's whisker. It's this knowledge more than anything else that helps me retain my calm in the face of the priest's gloating.

He leaves then and I'm left alone with my thoughts. A long time later the slave returns with my second meal of the day but she's alone this time and Meneth and I have no further conversation.

Downcast Dalila or The Trap Is Eluded

—Samson wake up! Dalila cried.—They're upon us a second time!

Somehow I had fallen asleep despite my efforts to remain vigilant. I didn't know how it could happen but there it was. The last thing I remembered was my and Dalila's coupling and then her offering me a goblet of wine. Despite my Nazirite vow I had allowed myself to take some for my thirst after sporting with Dalila was great indeed. The wine had spread across my tongue like a benediction but wine alone shouldn't have left me so dulled unless it was uncommonly potent. Well then—the LORD hadn't waited long to visit my punishment upon me.

—Quickly Samson! There are more of them this time and they've bound your wrists as before!

That was nothing. The hemp snapped like linen. These cords were newly woven but dry and they had no give to them. The disturbing thing was that I had told Dalila only the previous day that such could imprison me. Someone had been spying on us again and I was growing weary of it.

No time to wonder at that though. Once again I prayed thanks to God that I had thought to dissemble and tell Dalila a falsehood instead of the honest truth for these dried sinews were as nothing to me and I scattered them like chaff. And then I scattered the men as well. Dalila was right: there were more this time and the barn was a larger space where they had the advantage of cover and ambush but in the end it mattered not for I fought with the fury of the LORD upon me. And this time I left several of them alive and bleeding and praying for death but before granting it I questioned them with care. And so I hoped to learn more than before.

Alas I did not. Whoever had hired them hid his tracks well and I learned only that they had been recruited by a short dark man with a hook nose and a scar upon his forehead. Plus a mustache thick enough to sweep the floor with. He was not known to them as a military man or brigand or bandit of any stripe but he'd had cash and plenty of it which he paid out in advance. And thus did I learn what price was put on my head.

Despite myself I was impressed.—Am I really worth so much? I asked one of the wretches.

Blood spooled from his nose and mouth and turned the barn's dirt floor black.—Someone thinks so he said.

—What about your life? I demanded.—Is your life worth so much less than mine that you should sacrifice it so freely?

Whatever he answered came out only as bloody froth and I let the corpse drop.

Then was silence in the barn.

I scratched my head and looked around. Dalila was again dressed while I was naked and I admit for a moment some doubt passed over my mind like a cloud edging across the sun. Strange it was how we both fell asleep naked but she awoke clothed whereas I was bound and in the company of armed murderers. Doubtless you'll think me stupid indeed for not seeing the truth staring at me unblinking like an idol but all I can say in my defense was that I was blinded—both with animal lust and with some genuine stirrings of higher feeling—and if I saw only what I chose to see then I cannot be accused of being the first man who ever made that mistake.

Or the last.

—You are safe? I asked her.

—Yes she said.

But wait. There's more to it and I will admit this too. In the history of my people there are any number of influential women. This is but one more thing that sets us above the infidels. Sara and Rebecca are two such and I've always been an admirer of Debbora who did her best to unite the tribes of my people and brought them to battle the Canaanites who she cleverly lured to Mageddo. There the water flooded the valley and forced the heavy Canaanite chariots to withdraw and there did the infidel general Sisara seek refuge from a woman named Jahel. Whether she was Israelite I don't know but a friend to us she most surely was for she welcomed Sisara into her home before offering him butter and milk and then with a mallet drove a spike through his temple while he ate and thus the day was won. A most uncommon woman she must have been is what I've always thought. I would have liked to meet her.

What all these women had in common was their heritage. Philistine they were not and I must now confess that at the time Dalila busily plotted my downfall I had little belief in the ability of a woman and a heathen woman at that to act bravely enough to do me harm. Or in fact to take any kind of bold action for it's well known that Philistine women are passive downtrodden and lacking in vivacity or assertiveness. Which attitude was obviously shortsighted and ill considered but not uncommon amongst my people and I'm enough of a product of my people to share their bias and this I bring no shame in admitting for it's true of any man of whatever background including yourself.

—So then Dalila said in a hollow voice—This place is secret no longer.

—If it ever was I told her.—We've not been coming here for even a week.

I watched her closely: she wouldn't meet my eye. Her shoulders slumped in a manner unusual for her and I could see some of her spirit had gone. I could guess why too for I felt the same. Just that day Dalila had brought me a honey cake baked by her own hand (tasty it was too) and as we devoured it we spoke of my going to meet her father but obviously it wasn't safe. Exposing her family to this type of danger would be purely selfish and so arose the whole sticky issue once again of whether we should continue as we were or else walk away from each other while we still had the health to walk.

She stood watching me as if my thoughts were loud in her ears until the chin of Downcast Dalila started to tremble.

I sighed. Mighty as I was against a hundred armed men I had no defense against a lone woman's tears. Many would call this weakness and they'd be right. Others would call it I know not what. Humanity perhaps or compassion or any number of other words or maybe just kindness. Such things warriors are taught to scorn and maybe they're correct to do so or perhaps not I don't know. Such distinctions are beyond me. But when she looked upon me so the fear and hurt loomed plain in her eyes as if writ in words of fire large against the nighttime sky. And I resolved that this short woman who was maybe starting to love me a little and who I was maybe starting to love—not in that false phony way spoken of by fools but in a plain real earthy way involving flesh & food conversation & laughter—shouldn't be harmed by the wayward tides of violence in my life. And you may make of that what you will: kindness or weakness compassion or folly maturation or childishness.

Or all of these blended together with other things besides.

So I said—We must find yet another place.

—Oh she breathed and stepped towards me.

I held up my hand and she stopped.

Loudly I said—You know the stables by the market road where your father keeps his horses?

—Yes. She frowned. —But—

I held up a finger to my lips and squinted from side to side. Then I saw that she understood and nodded slightly. I said—very loudly for the sake of any listening ears—We will meet there at sunrise in three days' time.

She frowned but nodded.

—There's an empty stall at the far end as you enter. Bring a blanket and we will meet there.

—All right she said softly.

—Remember Dalila I said louder than ever.—The stable by the market road.

—In three days' time she repeated. Louder now.

And then I stepped to her and pulled her body close. It was soft against mine as she held herself against me and her curls still smelt of oil and I cupped her rump in my palms while she grasped my shoulders. Never had I been held so. For such a small woman she had a surprisingly tight grip and I thought if she clutched me any more fiercely she would leave welts.

—The river I whispered in her ear.—Tomorrow.

Tomorrow

But the next day I didn't go to the river. I had just said that to get Dalila out of harm's way. So while she waited as I supposed in some safe spot of her own choosing I went investigating which is no easy thing to do when you're as large as I am and not local and attention follows everywhere you go. But still there are always people ready to enhance their own standing by being seen with a great man even if he's no friend of theirs and thus it was in Sorec as elsewhere.

I began in the marketplace.—I'm looking for a man I said.—I don't know his name but he's small and dark.

—Small and dark? The wool merchant shrugged.—Oh well that narrows it down.

—With a big mustache I told the dyer.—And a hook nose.

—Ask Frem the dyer told me pointing to a leatherworker's stall.

—Small and dark I told the craftsman.—Big mustache & hook nose scar on his forehead & plenty of money to spend.

—Sounds like a servant this Frem opined. He was the kind of old man who knew everybody and spoke freely without worrying about who wouldn't like it.—Was the money his own or someone else's?

—I don't know I admitted.

—Well what was he buying?

—People—he was hiring people. Bodyguards. Armed men.

—Oh he was certainly a servant then. You'd never see a rich man out here talking to armed ruffians would you?

—I suppose not I said though in truth I had no idea what a Philistine would do or not do. To Frem I said—So to find this man.

—You'll need to ask at the big houses. Frem's leathery-brown fingers waved towards one corner of the city.—That way.

At that very moment Dalila herself was among those big houses but of course I didn't know that then. I wouldn't see her because she was careful to keep an eye out for me but if I had stumbled upon her maybe I'd've started to weave the basket together. I'm not saying it's sure just that I might have. What she was doing was meeting with her employers who were getting impatient with her and saying things like—Woman do you think you're toying with us? Think you this is some game?

—Of course not she snapped (or so I suppose she would've).—What do you expect? It's no easy task you've set.

—That's why you're getting paid they reminded her.—So that you might trap the man not so that we can sacrifice more of our own.

And another added—Twenty good men have died already due to your mistakes.

She'd've bristled at that. (There are some things I can't know but this I'm sure of.)—I remind you gentlemen that I was present at those battles and you were *not*. Your twenty so-called good men were killed by their own incompetence and impatience. More than that they were killed by a warrior who puts any of ours to shame. They were so busy stumbling backwards that half of them impaled themselves on the other half's weapons. Blame me not for their deaths—blame their own cowardly fumbling.

—Be that as it may the princes began. (For such is their manner of speech and though I loathe it I've heard plenty in my time to remember it so.)—Be that as it may the fact remains that our soldiers are dead while our quarry remains uncaught.

—You can always round up more ruffians.

—Yes we can said the oldest whose white hair was a thin ruff around the edge of his scalp. The tip of his nose bent down so far that it obscured his lips when he spoke.—But what about you Dalila? Can you do your job or are we to wait upon his convenience?

—I can do my job. You needn't worry.

—But we are worrying Dalila. That's the problem. And we shall not tolerate this situation for an indefinite period.

—Is that a threat? she sneered.

—Yes it is.

Silence in the chamber then. (For I imagine they were meeting in some grand chamber with screens in the windows and chairs and a table and—who knows—maybe even a rug. Or more than one. For the rich are ever partial to such excess.) The silence wasn't empty: it was filled with threat and tension and all the men enjoyed the satisfaction of watching Dalila taking in the man's words and pondering them. Just as she was about to speak the old one continued—With so many soldiers trailing you and Samson both it's no wonder if some mishap should occur. Even if he himself were to escape again. Well.

He shrugged. And said—Accidents happen. Blades flailing around in close quarters and you there half naked with no way to defend yourself. You poor dear. Daughter of Philistia and so forth. Our poets would compose dirges to your memory.

Dalila said nothing.

The old man squinted.—A shame indeed if this had to happen. See that it doesn't hmm?

Their conversation well and truly over Dalila turned to go. The princes watched with an odd mix of satisfaction at their bullying of the woman but fear that their plan wasn't working: after all I was still loose. They felt as if they'd accomplished something that day but were unsure how useful it would ultimately prove to be.

I knew none of this of course. In fact I still know none of this—I made much of it up. But from piecing together events later on I gathered that such a meeting as this took place sometime. This day when Dalila and I were apart was as likely a day as any. In the meantime I went looking for the short servant with the bushy mustache and a scar on his forehead with plenty of money to hire murderers to kill me and at length after much skulking about—not my best skill and never has been—I found him and surprised him on a footpath running away from the town. I mean the path was running not the man. He was ambling quite relaxedly as if pleased with his life and what he had made of it. I waylaid him and quickly ascertained that he was the man I was looking for hook nose and all. Although he was quite frightened he refused to tell me anything other than what I already knew: that he was the man who hired the murderers. Only he called them troops not bandits. Whatever. I could get nothing further from him as apparently his allegiance to his master was greater than that to his life. So after much fruitless questioning I grew impatient with him and wrung his neck which twisted and snapped just as several stalks of celery will do in the hands of a lesser man and I tossed him in the bushes beside the footpath and went looking for Dalila along the river knowing nothing more than I had the previous day.

Gossip

Meneth has been keeping his distance for the past week. I never expected to say this but I have grown to almost miss his presence. I don't mean that he is anything other than a repulsive lying heathen piece of offal but he also was someone to talk to—a voice in my all-consuming darkness—and for this I was I realize now inadequately grateful. And thus does the LORD even now chastise me for my faults and seek to improve His servant in tiny increments day by day. For whoever said that we never miss those things we have until they have been taken away spoke truer than he knew.

The real truth of course is that sooner or later everything is taken away.

One effect of Meneth's leaving is that I have no further window into the machinations of this great temple in which I'm chained. Now my only speech is with the jangling slave who brings me my food and when I speak to her (for still I hope it is the same tall dark woman as before) she only grunts in response or else says nothing at all as if afraid. Not that she has anything to fear of me but there you go. Habit runs deep I guess or maybe we are both closely watched by others beyond the reach of my senses. And though I have often benefited from the fear of others it's not the first time I can think of that this emotion has run counter to my interests. Often I've wondered what it would be like to be looked upon with something other than terror & apprehension foreboding & awe but I have come to realize that this is something I will never know.

I do however catch occasional snippets of conversation. After all I'm being held in the grandest chamber of the temple—or so I hope for I can't imagine any chamber bigger than this one. Since losing my sight I've remarked a great deal of activity: people bustling and clunking and knocking about from which I gather that furniture of some sort is being carried in and given the bits and pieces of conversation I've detected I have deduced that these are long tables and benches for what will be a great banquet. It seems the guests are to eat together in this hall with my execution for dessert. Or perhaps I'm to be the main course served up stuffed like a pig which the heathens find so delightfully tasty though it is an affront to the LORD Himself not to mention the intestines of any civilized man.

I'm speaking symbolically here. I don't expect the heathens to actually carve me up and serve me on a plate although with heathens you never know.

The number of diners seems to be enormous judging from the amount of furniture being brought in and the quantities of food being discussed. Entire herds of sheep harvests of wine and so on. There are also certain hushed tones used while discussing this or that eminent personage so I gather that what Meneth told me was right: all the highest families are sending their best. Really it's quite ironic if you think about it which is admittedly something I have too much time to do: the scourge of the Philistines being made into the center of their festivities.

Hundreds of people—too terrified to face me while I walked as free as they—jamming together into a single hall to dine with me safely in chains. Although I strive to honor the LORD with all my heart and always do His bidding yet do I wonder from time to time about His sense of humor. Or perhaps He's just reminding me to stay humble which is something—I know this—that I have trouble with. Or maybe there's something else. Maybe the LORD has a plan.

And maybe as ever I have a part in it.

I've grown weary of waiting for Meneth's pleasure so this evening when the servant brings me my slop I ask if she will run a comb through my hair.—It itches I whine in my most pitiful voice.

The servant hesitates then whispers—They might beat me.

I'm in luck: it's a woman's voice. The same woman or so I believe. I straighten my back a little and tell her—More likely they'll beat me. Please. On my honor I beg you.

This time her hesitation is briefer.—All right.

Few men would have agreed. But however many days I've been hanging here in chains my shoulders are still broad enough and my stomach flat enough and my chest expansive enough to catch the eye of nearly any woman child or crone. This is not boasting it's the truth. So when the servant returns after my wretched supper to run a rough wooden comb through my hair I know she does so with not a little excitement and—should she be married—I know perfectly well what will be playing in her mind the next time she lies with her husband. And thus do we find advantage in the most unexpected of places—such as the loins of a lonely long-since-bartered slave.

She rests the flat of her hand against my back as she tugs through the greasy knots. (Strictly speaking it's not necessary

that she place her hand there.)—That feels wonderful I say.—
Thank you.

In answer she barely murmurs something. Not even a whisper. More of a humming sound.

—What's your name? I ask. Not because I really care but because I want her to linger and talk. But she says nothing.

A few moments later I say again—That feels good. It's getting long isn't it?

By way of an answer her finger pokes into my back some distance below my neck.

—That long? I ask but she answers not. Just goes back to the slow patient rhythm of her combing.

It's longer than I thought but still I fear not long enough. How much more will it be allowed to grow? It seems inconceivable that Dalila never told the Philistines the details of my capture—that she just collected her money and left with no further conversation. Yet that was my impression at the time of my arrest and nothing since has altered it. More confusing still is my Philistine jailers' inability to weave the basket themselves: a mighty warrior with much hair becomes a weak prisoner with none. How are they so stupid as to overlook the obvious? Maybe it's just a case of being too close to something to see the truth of it.

Or maybe yet something else. Maybe Dalila misled them by saying—The power of my loins has tamed him. It sucked all his strength away and left him weaker than a woman. This would've gotten her a big laugh from the princes and maybe no little respect too. It might've made it easier to hand her such vast sums of silver. In which case my shorn hair would be seen as merely one humiliation among many.

This idea holds a certain logic though I admit logic is no specialty of mine.

There is another possibility too: that Dalila was presenting me with a chance however slim to bide my time and escape. To which I can hear you ask:—Why would she do so? Did she have feelings for you Samson? Was there some part of her that was woman enough to overlook her duty to her nation and her employers and see you only as a man and a lover and not such a terrible one at that?

I believe there was. My feelings for her I've made no attempt to hide. It's reasonable to think they could be returned however imperfectly.

So then. The more I think on this the more it makes sense: that her silence was in fact Dalila's final gift to me.

To the slave who still combs my hair I say—Tell me do you know when this banquet is going to take place?

At this she stops abruptly.—I shouldn't be here she mumbles before shuffling off.

—Wait! I call out but she's gone. I've learned some of what I need however. Not all of it: I still don't know when the banquet is planned. I don't know the date of my presumed execution or how much time I have to prepare.

Somehow though I think I will have enough.

You Will Be Forgiven at This Point for Thinking I'm Really Very Stupid

I waited at Dalila's father's stables three days after the second ambush. You'll remember that I had thought to trick my attackers into seeking me there and I planned to slay them all but one or two and then set about questioning them not stopping until I had the information I wanted. I would threaten their children & hack off fingers gouge their eyes & do whatever was needed. Of course none of it happened because they'd been informed that the sunrise meeting at the stables was a ruse.—Someone's told them I said to Dalila later that day—not realizing that I was speaking to the person in question.

Tender Dalila was back and her face looked stricken.—I fear for you Samson.

So did I a little. To be honest these repeated ambushes were making me weary. But retreating now would've been an affront to my pride that I was unready to accept. More than anything I wished to track down these killers and finish them off once and for all. If you wish to fault me for this stubbornness you are free to do so. But if I had fled Gaza there are many who would find fault in my cowardice and maybe you would be one of *those* too.

Moreover there was a part of me that didn't want to appear a coward in front of Dalila. If this pride is a sin then I'm guilty for I valued her good opinion and wished to appear brave & manly strong & unfrightened in her eyes. And thus do our shortcomings lead us invariably to our doom.

To soothe her I played down my concerns saying only— Let's continue our meetings here on the riverbank. It's a good place far away from the town and nobody will know.

She glanced around.—A little exposed no?

—Come here I said.

A curious thing had happened during these three days we had been apart. I found my mind occupied with Dalila very much as if she had been there with me. Apart from the men I sought who had been trying to kill me I thought of little else. Hearing a bird I wondered if Dalila would recognize its song.

Tasting a stew I thought that Dalila could cook a spicier one. Gazing at the twilight I wondered whether she looked upon the same colors. And so on. I even invented little conversations in my head and played them out over and over.

Despite my lack of experience with such musings I could guess what they signified. I had seen more than one lovestruck youth sighing over his neighbor's daughter to recognize these signs in me. More than that I was happy about it—which any man can tell you is a symptom that the disease has progressed well past its initial stages.

Now I led her into a little glade where an enormous hemlock grew up like a tent with thick branches lowering down to the ground like the skirts of an old woman. Inside was a roomy chamber quite invisible to the outside world and soft underfoot with hemlock needles piled up in layers as thick as your fist. Birds chirruped overhead invisibly. Green shadows fell thick over everything.—Well? I said.

She smiled slyly.—And how many others have you taken to this place?

—None I said and laid her down.—And none after you either. For this was true: it was strong in my mind that after Dalila I would need no other woman. I even said as much. She had been so out of sorts from these recent attacks that I wished to please her and make her smile and so she did and I was glad. Then I went in her.

Afterwards we lay and watched the creatures scampering through the boughs overhead. She shifted in the crook of my arm and then again and yet again and I knew she was building up to something. For Dalila was a woman whose restless thoughts were made plain by the restlessness of her body. For the most part this liveliness pleased me.

I said nothing knowing it would come soon enough. And so it did.—Samson she said—I've been thinking about these attacks.

—Me too.

—And I'm thinking that if I knew your vulnerabilities I would be better able to help you.

—Mm hm?

—Consider a moment she said.—If I knew what made you weak I could better place myself to prevent that from ever happening.

I tried not to laugh but couldn't help smiling.—Dalila I said—you've got skills unlike any woman I've ever known and I've known a few. But fighting is something I think I can do without the assistance of a naked unarmed woman who barely reaches my chest.

She pulled away at that and left space between us. Not a great deal of space but some. And I knew it was up to me to close that gap. I had missed her lately—but I had missed Sweet Dalila and Eager Dalila not Ranting Dalila or Needy Dalila. Now that we were back together and the sun lingered on our bodies I didn't want some annoying scene. So I said—Listen. It's my hair.

She said nothing.

I had never gotten this close to revealing myself to anyone so I chose my words with care.—My hair is the source of both my strength and my vulnerability.

She half leaned back to half look at me.—Your hair?

—Just so.

She was thoughtful a moment.—For some reason that's not surprising. Tell me.

—If it's plaited—like this yes?—into braids and wrapped

around an iron spike and then that spike is jammed into the ground I will be immobilized and weak as a kitten.

She frowned at this.—A very odd vulnerability isn't it?

I rolled my eyes.—You'd prefer something different? The smell of boiled eggs maybe?

She pinched my arm.—I didn't say *that* she giggled.— Though now that you mention it—

—None of this was my idea you know. I just have to live with it.

Some part of me half expected to wake up the next day to find my hair plaited and tied to an iron spike pounded into the ground but it didn't happen. Nor the day after that nor again the next. Then Dalila began her unclean time and said she was in pain—for so it happened sometimes—and for some days I didn't see her and images of her again filled my thoughts. Not just her bosoms and ankles and hips but her face too—her even white teeth with the little space in the middle and her voice and the lines that crinkled out from her eyes when she laughed. Also the eyebrows. It was interesting how I noticed these things. When again we met I was hungry for her and had all but forgotten our conversation so when she started teasing me how I would look better this way or that I never gave it much thought.

One afternoon she presented me with a bangle. Thick iron and snake-shaped the snake swallowing its tail. I didn't like it for it reminded me of the idols of the heathens but I thanked her for it anyway and resolved never to wear it.

—Wear it she wheedled so I did.

Other things followed. A fashion at that time was for the high-born young men to wear earrings of colored stones much as women did and though I never wanted any part of such nonsense Dalila pressed and pressed until finally I poked the stud through my ear though I tore it out again the moment we parted. Then there were the tattoos such as sailors wear—a line of dots along the forearm—that I flatly refused and any number of pointless frivolities. Most were harmless enough such as wearing closed boots instead of simple open sandals or colorful squares of cloth draped from one's belt but I was comfortable with few of them and pleased with none. I kept the bangle she gave me that first time but had no truck with any of the others and all her pleading failed to dissuade me. And then she started in on my hair.

—There's a fashion these days for the men to cut it short she announced one afternoon.

Well as you can imagine such talk left me cold. So I said—You can forget about that for I will never cut it.

—Why not? she asked.—It's so ragged and lank it reaches halfway down your back.

—God willing it will remain so I said.

—Does it mean that much to you?

I was reluctant to go into the whole history of my hair and the Nazirites and my oath and so on. Although I trusted Dalila I didn't trust whoever might hear of it through her and besides I had long been in the habit of keeping that part of my life hidden. Whether anyone could have guessed the secret of my strength after learning of my oath I didn't know and was in no hurry to discover. So I said merely—Let's have no more of this talk for I'm fond of my hair and want no man to touch it.

—All right she pouted.—Then at least let me do something about your beard.

For you will recall that I never shaved my whiskers and my

beard was a thick tangle indeed that hung from my face like some shrubbery. But still this was as much a part of my strength as my hair was so I was no happier to countenance cutting it either. So I grumbled—Leave it be. What's wrong with it anyway?

—Oh Samson it's a mess. And she ran her fingers through it until they caught in the snags which was almost immediately.—See? she said.—At least let me comb it.

This I let her do and it was no pleasure. She used a broad-toothed wooden comb of the sort used for carding wool and I had pity for those sheep then. In her defense Dalila took great care and more time than any other woman would have—apart of course from my dear mother Sala—and when she was finished my beard fell with a smoother grace than before and even a certain softness. She took it on herself to oil it as well and then the shine and luster were something to see all right. All this took the better part of an afternoon but I had to admit that when she was done I looked quite tidy.

—There she said.

She patted my beard and gave me such a smile that an odd swelling feeling expanded inside me—not in my loins but behind my stomach somewhere—and I believe I looked upon her with love. For some moments I could hardly speak. Then I managed to say—Better? though it came out more like the croak of a frog than any human speech.

—Better.

I should've known it wouldn't end there. Next she begged to tie little braids among the fibers of my beard and to thread cowries amid it which I grudgingly conceded to. However when it came to the matter of adding small yellow flowers I flatly refused. But she did enough of the other that I looked a plain fool much of the time and tore out her little bejewelments as soon as possible.

The she started in with my hair again and I let her comb and oil it and when she was done I admit it looked quite grand. (Though also rather feminine but I thought: *I can ignore this*.) But when she brought up the matter of trimming it I roared—No! And I will hear no more of this understand?

—All right she sulked.

—I am tired of all this. Promise me you won't bring the matter up again.

—I promise she said.—I promise you Samson: no man shall ever touch your hair.

And I believed her. And typical of Dalila she found a way to keep true to the letter of her promise while yet finding a way to do exactly as she pleased. Wench.

Playful Dalila or The Trap Is Reset

Some days after this Dalila tied my hair back in a series of thick braids.—If I can't cut it she said—at least let me plait it and get it out of your face so I can see you.

I was sick unto death of arguing so I humored her and I admit when she was done my head felt surpassingly light and my view was unobstructed and my neck was less sweaty and any other number of pleasant effects could be noted. So I told her—Thank you. I didn't expect to like it but I do.

She smiled at that and lines crinkled out from her eyes once again stoking my fondness for her. Then we lay together and I went in her.

Afterwards I lay on my back while she massaged my scalp.

Through half-closed eyes I squinted at the hemlock overhead and the sun slanting through it in the late afternoon where flocks of waxwings and finches squabbled for territory—for so is humanity's image reflected in the habits of the lower creatures—with the occasional squirrel bustling through it all. My mind started to play upon the many ways that animals are just like people and then that thought transformed itself into how often people act just like animals and then I felt myself at the verge of some stark revelation when suddenly I realized that Dalila was no longer massaging my scalp but instead had gathered my plaited braids of hair together and was doing something with them. Pulling on them in a strange twisting fashion and then a sharp tug as they were pushed or nailed or pounded into the earth. And a hard kernel of doubt and accusation grew solid within me but before I could speak she leaned over me her face upside down above mine with her teats soft and heavy against my forehead and she leaned down to kiss me and her face felt strange but also pleasing upside down and her bosoms were warm.

She broke off and said—Now we shall have a game all right?

—What is it?

—The game is that you have to do whatever I tell you.

—We play that one already.

Her smile twisted at one corner.—Ha ha she said.—This game is different. In this game you're helpless because I've nailed your plaits into the ground with an iron spike so you have no strength left so you have to do everything I say.

—I don't like this game I said.

—If you don't like it then we shall only play this one time.

—Promise?

—Oh yes.

All at once there came a crashing and stomping through the

underbrush and the footsteps and cries of many men. Dalila whose face still hung over mine looked around wildly and hissed—They are upon us Samson! before rearing backwards and out of my sight. I sensed her cowering terrified behind my prone form and even as the footsteps rumbled closer and dark shapes grew heavy through the veils of hemlock needles I sat upright tearing the iron spike from the ground and shaking my head to free the plaits. Braided or no I still had my hair and thus my strength. The spike I used as a missile to lance the first one's sternum and as he fell to the earth clawing himself I hefted his sword and had at the others.

It was less of a fight than the first two: most of the men turned and ran when they saw me on my feet. Again I was left with only one half-dead survivor to interrogate and again he didn't look as though he would last long.

He was the lead attacker with the spike in his ribs. The iron was as long as my hand and the man was dying fast but I admit to some grudging admiration for his courage in flinging himself at me headlong and at the fire of defiance that burned in him even as his life ebbed. His hair was tight and curly though gray at the temples and his teeth were brown where they weren't entirely black. Still his eyes shone clear enough and when I said—Tell me who sent you he spit back—Can't you guess?

I hefted the sword over his prone form.—Speak fast I've no time for riddles.

—As if I do he coughed. Blood oozed from his chest in slow thick pulses.

—How did your men know where to find me? I pressed.

—They're led here you stupid fool by that slut of yours. She tells them everything.

From behind me a gasp. I didn't turn but I knew Dalila was listening and could imagine the look of distress on her face.

—Speak the truth I told the man—and you may yet live a few moments more.

He laughed or rather tried to.—What are a few moments? I speak the truth because it suits me to. This poxy shrew is in the service of the princes who pay her to find your secrets and pass them along. This harlot—this harpy—this siren—this harridan was supposed to have saved the lives of myself and my men and God knows how many dozens of others. Instead she cavorts with you till her cunt runneth over while we are led into trap after trap like sacrificial virgins.

This was some high-class language for a simple bandit I thought to myself. And fine names to be calling the woman I was starting to love or so I thought. My fists clenched though I as yet held myself in check.

Panting hard Dalila was beside me now.—You lying bastard!

But the man didn't stop.—She consults with them every few days and they must be getting impatient by now. She's made a fist of things what—three times now? Four? And the bodies keep piling up. The princes are starting to threaten her and there's some who think the whole plan should be scrapped in favor of the direct approach. And the old man he's not happy at all.

—What old man? I asked.

—The one she reports to his name is—

With a howl Dalila fell upon the wretch. She produced a small knife from I know not where and used it expertly and the man's throat was open and his voice stilled forever.

I watched her as she straightened up her fast shallow breaths becoming slower. She seemed reluctant to look at me but after a time collected herself to say—Forgive my outburst. I couldn't bear any more of his lies.

—Of course I said.

She looked at me then.—They were lies you know. You know that don't you? What better way to distract you from the real threat than to put the blame on me? On someone who wants only the best for you?

I nodded. To be honest I wasn't sure: my thoughts and feelings bubbled together and tumbled against each other like lentils in a pot. But gradually I sorted through them and saw that her words made sense. In the soldier's place I'd've done the same thing.

—It's all right I said—I believe you. He was just—talking. Trying to confuse me. Yes. Throw me off the track.

She wrapped her arms round me then and burrowed her face into my chest.—It's important to me that you believe that.

—I do I said. And then again a little louder and stronger because the first time it had come out uncertain:—I do.

Preparations

The temple is crowded now. The guests have been arriving for some days. They mill around and draw near sometimes while I sleep and when I wake and raise my head the intake of their surprised breath is like the wind passing outside a window at night. Not a storm exactly but building up to one. Most of them disperse but there are always a few who stand by and discuss me as if I'm deaf as well as blind.

—Dun't look like much does he?

—You wun't say that if you'd saw what he done to Glef.

What is Glef I wonder to myself. A man? A village? For in my time I've destroyed plenty of both and I wouldn't hesitate to do so again. If called upon of course.

—My cousin lived there with his family the voice goes on—and his wife's family as well. This son of a whore arrives one morning and torches the whole place. Kills 'em all children too. Salts the fields. Tears out the olives. He's a monster this one dun't you doubt it.

—Kills the children you say?

—Burnt 'em in their huts. Those left alive starved to death anyway so no difference I can see.

Such things they say about me you hear them for yourself. Not lies exactly but incomplete truth which is anyway no better than a lie. This is why I've chosen to tell my own story for my own sake—so that the truth can be known or at least my life as I understand it. Well do I know that when I'm gone (and my time is coming soon there's no point denying this) such lies and calumny will be spread about me that the truth will be a difficult thing to perceive in amongst all the falsehoods like a small precious stone dropped in a toilet pit.

Another voice says—What I wouldn't give to see this bastard crawl.

—You'll see it soon enough answers yet another.

—And more than that says a third. An old man's voice this is—squawky and dry like some he-goat on its last legs.—What say we have him dance for us?

—Yes! Har! they bay like whelps.—Dance fucker dance!

There is a sharp crack against the back of my knee and I jerk away from the pain which is sharp and stinging. Howls and hoots of derision greet my movement and another whizzing slap slams the back of my other knee and of course

I reel away in the opposite direction. With the chains tight against my wrists I'm unable to do more than twist this way and that like a doll in some furious child's hands but this is just what the crowd is looking for.

—Dance! Dance you sisterfucker!

The jangling of my manacles as I jerk back and forth is the only accompaniment. This goes on for a long time and is more painful than I care to admit. I've been left hanging here for weeks and my shoulders are by now permanently cramped and moaning and this lurching back and forth does nothing to lessen the agony. I fear I even make groans and grunts of pain as I thrash about which excites the crowd into a positive frenzy. It's only when I grow exhausted and stop moving despite their ever-harder jabs and pummelings that they grow bored and drift away. I'm left hanging on my chains like some half-dead thing: some offering or pathetic piece of meat hung like a carcass in a butcher's stall.

Which if I allow myself to think on it too much is more or less what I've been reduced to.

I Reveal My Secret to Dalila for Reasons That Will Probably Not Satisfy You but Which Are the Only Reasons I Have

After our latest attack there came a period of time that would change things forever between Dalila and me. Dalila seeing how weary I was of her constant questioning pressed me all the harder and demanded & wheedled coaxed & begged sniffled & joked all to find out the secret source of my power. She said things like—Don't you know I would do anything for you Samson? You saw me kill that man with your own eyes! and much else besides which rather than bringing clarity left me more puzzled and uncertain than ever. Besides this she grew reluctant to leave my side and kept always near me saying—I can't let you go—your enemies are everywhere! which after a time led me confusedly to believe that she was empowered to protect me not the other way round.

Moreover she never let me rest.—Sleep not Samson she urged—for when you slumber your enemies come near and since you'll not let me know the secret of your strength then I can't protect you when you lie so naked and vulnerable.

All of which kept me muddled particularly after the third day and the fourth without sleep and it seemed Dalila's only interest apart from keeping me awake was coupling with me. Which we did often and I heartily enjoyed but it also left me wearier than ever and although it's an activity a man can perform readily enough for a time without rest—sooner or later he needs to lay his head somewhere. But Dalila connived to prevent this.

—You must keep your wits about you she said.—But if you like I can comb your hair.

—All right.

This was something she did now with frequency and I had grown to like it. I won't lie: I had grown to enjoy it nearly as much as lying with her. But in a different way. For she would sit me up and kneel behind and her bosoms would press against my shoulders comfortingly as she ran her fingers through my hair which she now kept regularly oiled. (I wouldn't allow the perfume she begged to add as well.) The comb's teeth against my scalp felt refreshing and her fingers tugging the lengths of the strands soothed me and it must be confessed that often at such times I was reminded of my mother Sala who regularly performed this same chore in my childhood. I don't mean any perversity by this or that Sala was undressed when so doing or that I ever wanted to go into my own mother. Merely that the tug and stroke along my head soothed and took me back to that time before my life grew heavy with blood.

I have observed many times that a mother cat will carry her kittens by the neck and when this happens even the liveliest of them grows docile and slack in her jaws. Something similar happened to me whenever Dalila leaned me against her bosom and ran the comb through my hair and her fingers played across my scalp like a flute. For truly I was a flute at such moments. And Dalila played me as skillfully as any musician.

—Does that feel nice? she always asked.

—Yes. Yes it does. Mmm.

Finally she wore me down. There's no more to it than that: I'm a strong man but she wore me down. Which I suppose speaks much about her own strength. Even the rocks along the shore given enough time and pressure from the waves will turn to sand. Thus does the LORD give us beaches to walk upon and launch our boats from to journey into the sea and catch fish. Come to think of it this is something the Philistines excel at so maybe that was the plan all along: to turn mighty Samson into a beach by wearing him down bit by bit and so they did.

—My hair I whispered one day as she sat combing it. She had just asked me the secret of my strength and I told her.

—Yes yes she said absently. We were sitting again in the

clearing beneath the hemlock. There seemed no point in moving since we were always found wherever we went. I was leaning against Dalila's heavy breasts as she ran the comb almost lazily along my scalp.—You said your hair before she said.—Plaits and spikes and all the rest. You lied to me three times already so don't expect me to smother you with gratitude now.

My eyes were closing of their own accord. I felt heavy in the head as if I had been beaten by strong men.—No plaits I said.—No spikes. My hair has never felt the bite of a razor nor my beard either. It is my testimony before God. When it grows I have strength. If it were ever shaved I would be weak as any man.

I felt the comb stop moving. Then start again but slower. Her voice sounded from a great distance as if from the bottom of a well or a distant hillside:—Is this the truth Samson?

—It is.

—I don't believe you she said. The comb matched the rhythm of her words. She said—Swear it before your God.

—I swear I said. So tired I felt at the very edge of death itself.—Before the LORD Himself I swear that my words are true.

She slid back a space and laid my head upon her lap with her arms cradling me. I felt childlike. I felt like a baby. Dalila's teats pressed into my face and her lap was warm against my cheek. The smell of her loins was like wet hay in my nostrils. For a moment I felt a hot trickle of desire but it was quickly extinguished by fatigue.

—Sleep she said.—I shall protect you. Sleep now.

Her fingers stroked my hair.

I slept. For the last time in my life—I slept in peace.

Entertainments

And who do you think puts an end to the daily entertainment of my unseen crowd of tormentors? None other but the supercilious priest Meneth that's who.

I will admit to a degree of gladness at his return. For although Meneth is no friend neither has he gone out of his way to be unkind. Unless you count his verbal taunting which to me is altogether different from physical cruelty.

So then I am delivered. However this doesn't happen before I've spent a good several days dancing in agony for my snickering audience of curs & serpents jackals & sheep buzzards & swine. And not before they grow increasingly bold and inventive in their torments. Hot coals placed on my unsuspecting feet draw appreciative giggles and for sheer unexpected meanness nothing can beat the jab against the kidneys with a sharpened stick or iron poker. Unless it is the jab against the loins with the same choice of implements. And so day by day I'm harried and weakened till I begin to wonder whether I will survive long enough to see my plans—tenuous as ever but slowly taking on clearer form in my mind's eye—come to pass.

And then one morning Meneth is there clearing away the crowd with a firmness that borders on being rude. When they're gone I say—Thank you.

—Don't thank me he purrs.—Plenty of important people are expected for your demise. Letting you curl up and expire before they're ready to witness it is simply not *on*.

You see? No friend is he but then again neither does he encourage pain for its own sake.

I say no more but offer gratitude only to the LORD for clearly this is His doing. Even the heathens bow to His will though they're too blind & stupid ignorant & proud to see it.

Meneth says—I see you've gotten someone to comb your hair at last. Feeling better?

—Yes I say.—The slave did it and its torment is much less. I've given up on the bath I add—though given my stench this probably troubles you almost as much as me.

He chuckles but says no more.

We stand there almost like companions who've had an argument but are getting past it. After a time I ask him—When do you expect this grand banquet? There are more people here than before if I'm not mistaken.

—So there are. But also many who haven't yet arrived. Don't worry—you'll have sufficient time to ahh contemplate your past crimes and regret them.

Regrets I have none but Meneth's not lying about the wait. Days pass and then more—stretching into weeks as I remain there strung up between the pillars. The heathens have ceased taking me back to my underground cell as they were doing at first. Now I'm on display at all hours. But an odd and unbelievable thing happens as I stand with my arms manacled and outstretched and I choke down the swill that is still brought to me twice daily by my silent fellow prisoner and my sleep continues to be interrupted by stray taunts and violent dreams. Something happens which is just about the last thing I expect or I'm sure anyone else does.

I grow stronger.

This is true I know because I can feel it. Hair hangs thick between my shoulder blades by now and as this wellspring of my power grows longer I can feel strength pulsing in my sinews. Layering up like bricks piling into rows to create an ever higher wall. If I drop my chin to my breastbone I can feel my beard's fingers tickling my nipples. Need I mention that these whiskers are growing far quicker than normal? As they grow I feel energy coursing through my limbs: already my shoulders and biceps which should be cramped and immobile are hurting less than before and it's easier to hold myself upright all day and night. At times I feel a slight flush burning behind my forehead and it's obvious at such moments that the LORD has turned His gaze upon me and is urging me not to lose heart. I'm not one to argue with Him so I do as I'm told.

Whether this change is visible to the outward eye I can't say but I notice that the taunts and jeers of my oppressors grow fewer as the days pass as if my improved condition is being noticed. Which just goes to show that a bully prefers to kick a victim who's already down but then that's common knowledge without my repeating it.

Once more I'm struck by the dullness of the heathen mind and its inability to see the connection between my power and my hair. But maybe I shouldn't be surprised for what other man in all human history can claim such?

Meneth for one isn't impressed.—Enjoy your second wind while you can he advises sourly.—Your destiny is fast approaching.

—I'm glad to hear it I say. And this time my boastful words are backed up with confidence that is genuine. I tell him—For my destiny is something I'm ready for.

Meneth—I sense this—squints at me quizzically.—You seem different.

—That I am. You'll see just how different in a few more days.

—If you have that long he grunts.—If I were you I would

make my peace with your so-called creator for soon enough
you'll be ahh meeting him face-to-face.

—I've made my peace long since I say.

A pause then as if Meneth wants to say something. I wait.
But after a time he moves off with no further word and I'm left
once more with the uncertainties of the future and my memories of the past.

Victorious Dalila or The Trap Is Sprung

This will be no surprise to you I suppose but it was quite
a surprise to me when I woke up and all the hair was shorn from
my head and my cheeks as well. Not that I realized so at the first
instant. For I woke startled to Dalila's shrieking and for many
confused blurry moments that's what concerned me.

—Samson wake up! They're here yet again!

Sometimes I have a dream that occurs over and over. Usually it takes place in my village of Dan where my parents'
homestead is engulfed in a fire I can never prevent no matter
how many times I witness it happening. Each time I'm
doomed to watch Sala and Manue char to blackened cinders
while I look on unable to move. Well that was the feeling I was
starting to get with these episodes—even though they actually
happened they brought to me upon waking that same bleary
feeling of unreality & repetition impotence & futility.

—Samson they're upon us!

So I jumped to my feet and rushed towards the shadowy fig-
ures hunkered outside the hemlock faintly sensing the chill
against my head and the lightness to my step and the coldness
on my throat and cheek but not thinking clearly about it—

wanting only to smash these same endless idiot men who threw themselves in front of me to die over and over before finally—and this time I swore it to myself—I would clear off from this cursed valley forever and return to my people where I belonged. And Dalila would come with me and I would tell her of my plans as soon as I was done with this. If she wished of course. I would leave it to her to accompany me if she so desired.

Alas.

The captain of this troupe of bandits was short and thickset like a block of stone with a stupid iron helmet that glowed dully in the forest. As I charged bellowing towards him I saw fear writ plain on his face like words of fire against the nighttime sky. I swung my arm roundhouse fashion to hurl his head back and snap his neck with little fuss and he raised his own stubby arm to parry my blow and did so—my arm striking weakly against his and bouncing off. Both of us were left standing unbalanced but upright and him with his mouth open looking as surprised as I.

—Eh?

He recovered first his expression changing from fear to delight and swung his short blunt sword and I fended off his attack with my arm but the pain of doing so wrenched my elbow and bounded up my shoulder like a swarm of wasps and dug in behind my eyes and in my teeth and brought me to my knees.

On my knees I looked up at him and he stared down at me.

—Well fuck me up the ass he said softly. The way he spoke it sounded like a prayer. Behind me Dalila inhaled suddenly and loud. The bandit looked past me to where she stood. He grinned like a lopsided wolf and said—You've done well sister.

It went badly for me after that.

I'm Arrested and Beaten

They brought me before their council of princes such as they called it but they were nothing so grand as the name suggests. Unlike my people the Philistines had no consistent system of law but only local rulers who fought amongst themselves as much as with us and when the need of the moment required them to work together they did so which is what had happened now. As for royalty they merely had families that were more influential than others by virtue of their wealth. Which come to think of it is maybe the only foundation that royalty is ever built upon. Anyway it was before these families that I found myself—or more rightly before the old men who controlled them and the young men who hungered after the position of the old men. So in a way you could say I was brought before princes but if you said I was brought before a cabal of leeches & jackals vultures & other scavenging beasts you wouldn't be far wrong either.

Before I got there I had to endure the kicks & punches slaps & pokes spitting & whipping of every ruffian in the group who captured me. Which were many. And then as I was led—staggering in chains amidst the great parade of howling sinners through the lanes of the valley—I had to endure it all again from the townsfolk. A huge train of laborers & farmers children & wives grew up behind me as I stumbled through the town barely able to totter upright so badly had I been beaten. And so severely had my eyes been jabbed by the bandits who called themselves soldiers that I could barely see and even as I made my way my vision was dimming under the brilliant noontime glare. A particularly vicious chop to the side of my head and I heard something snap and my right eye blurred and faded even more. And so began the failure of my eyesight which has ended in my blindness here in this temple.

In a way it was just as well for this meant I didn't have to look either upon the faces of my enemies or that of Dalila— who kept her distance some paces behind me and who I by then had guessed was just another enemy. This realization took some time to settle in and plenty bewildering it was too. But the taunts of the crowd made sure that I understood soon enough.

—There he is! See him! Brought low by a whore's cunning!

—Whore's cunting you mean.

—I wonder what she got for her trouble?

—Whatever it was wasn't enough.

—Tell you one thing she got—him! Five times a day is what I heard. Imagine lying with him for weeks just to get his secret—that tiny snip of a thing. And then bringing down the mightiest warrior who ever walked!

—Well he ain't the first imbecile to follow his cock to ruination.

—Tell him sister!

I will admit that at this point there were tears tracking their way down my cheeks but these were not tears of sadness or love betrayed. Or not mainly. They were tears of fury and physical pain as my abused eyes worked to protect themselves as best they could and my tormented soul loosed its frustration like a crack in the earth venting steam. But the crowd of course saw things differently.

—Wouldja lookit that! Crying for the slut!

—Hey Samson she was just the hired help!

—He wants to cry then he should cry for the innocents he's slaughtered.

Too dispirited even to yell back I merely walked with my head as high as I could hold it which I admit was not very.

At length I was brought into a small room with one big window spilling brilliant sunshine across the floor that made my vision even worse while the shadows pooled out from the corners to lick like tongues across the middle of the scene. There were bandits all around me in a crowd at my back—I never got a clear look at them but I would guess at least thirty. In front of me were five or six self-important men in robes of various colors that I couldn't focus on too well and as for their faces they were lost to me as any more than smears. Still it was easy enough to pick out their voices and imagine how they carried themselves. There was the Old Man in Charge and the Challenger and the Young Snake and the Fearful Braggart and a couple of others.

The Fearful Braggart spoke first.—So this is him? He doesn't look like much.

—Why didn't you catch him then? hissed the Young Snake.—Saved us all a lot of trouble.

The Fearful Braggart said no more.

The Challenger said—What's the plan then? I say we cut his throat and be done with it.

—We all know what you want said the Young Snake.—But things don't always go just how you want do they?

—What's that supposed to mean?

The Old Man in Charge cut them off.—Quiet both of you. We've discussed this and we shall act as we have decided. This—man—here has caused enough strife amongst our people we don't need him causing more now.

A moment's pause then the Young Snake:—To the temple then Uncle?

—Yes. To Gaza.

And so it was I learned of my destination: the temple of Dagon in Gaza—a place I had seen from the outside but never stepped into. Its immensity and heathen grandeur were plain to see from far off and it was spoken of with wonder even in my homeland. I had little hope then and I admit that I felt despair opening up beneath me like a chasm. No prisoner brought to Dagon's temple ever walked away again and I had no reason to expect myself the first.

—I still don't like this spoke up the Challenger.—There's too much that can go wrong and this creature has found ways in the past to exploit situations even when they looked bleak.

—He looks helpless enough to me opined the Fearful Braggart.

—Maybe so said the Challenger.—But I would remind you all that Dalila was hired only to capture him and bring him to us and she has done so. It is now our responsibility to keep him bound and I for one think we would be fools to underestimate him.

Even in my exhausted state my attention was nipped by this. They talked as if the secret of my weakness wasn't plain for all to see.

Maybe it wasn't. Maybe Dalila hadn't told them. At that I wondered *Why not?* and as you know this question has been much on my mind since then.

The Old Man's voice:—You are pleased to call me a fool then?

After some silence the Young Snake prompted the Challenger—My uncle asked you a question.

Another moment's pause and then another.—I'm calling no one a fool. But I—

The Old Man's voice took on the rhythms of a man giving a speech which I suppose is what he was at that moment. He said—This is not Jawbone I assure you. There will be no miraculous escape this time. The once mighty Samson has been emasculated: robbed of his strength and bound hand and foot. The witch Dalila has employed her female arts to render him helpless. I for one thank her for it and will be happy to see her paid and released from service.

Mumbled agreement from the crowd.

—Moreover went on the Old Man in Charge—we have righteousness on our side. The laws of nature as well as the fury of Dagon strengthen our arm. Does anyone doubt the sanctity of our cause?

Well that shut up the Challenger all right. I could sense the mass of armed men in the room throwing their approval behind the Old Man's word and why not? For after all nothing appeals to the heathen's uncivilized sensibility more than a blood sacrifice in the name of his god.

Whether this was the Old Man's reasoning or whether he himself was truly a fanatic who yearned to see me on the altar I couldn't say then and I still can't now. But the Fearful Braggart was quick to walk in the Old Man's footprints saying:—And when we have him at the temple then we will slice his throat!

I wondered who was this *we* that he spoke of so eagerly.

Not that I wondered long for the Old Man said—More than that we shall do. When one has one's fiercest enemy in hand one doesn't squander the opportunity to make an impression on both friends and foes.

The silence that greeted this declaration was the quiet of uncertainty: the silence of confusion. Clearly the Old Man in Charge had a plan in mind but no one else knew what it entailed. I didn't know any more than did the others of course. But I had a feeling that whatever it was it wouldn't be to my liking.

I'm Taken to Gaza

My transport to Gaza was unremarkable enough if you overlook the fact that it took place at all. I was bound and gagged and thrown atop a camel and carried there: all this taking far longer than it should because the parade traveled slowly giving every Philistine along the way opportunity to shower me with jeers and spittle. Ringed as I was by a phalanx of soldiers there was no way I could've escaped even had I been able to loose my bonds—which was well beyond me—but my escort did do me the favor of ensuring that I wasn't torn apart by the mob which I've no doubt would have happened otherwise. And though I did experience moments of black despair on that journey I will not test your patience by saying such things as *I prayed for death* and *It would've been better to let the mob have me* because never did I think such things. Beaten as I was I wasn't yet overwhelmed nor had I relinquished faith that the LORD had plans for me and had only allowed these events to occur because it suited Him to do so.

If Dalila came to Gaza I know nothing of it. I've not seen her since Sorec and don't expect to either. I feel no sadness at this point nor any sentimental nonsense about what might have been: only rage at my own stupidity. At times I wish my stupidity was a living man so I could cleave its skull and dump its life onto the ground and beat it with a stick but alas as we all know it's not like that and so every man must live with the foolishness of his past actions walking alongside him like his closest companion.

However I will admit even now to a grudging respect for Dalila. For truly she outwitted me and there are few warriors who won't acknowledge a superior who has proved himself— or herself—in the field. Besides this the memory of her loins remains sweet. I'm not especially proud of this but it's the truth so I lay it before you. Judge me if you will but remember as you do that you were never in my position and so never faced the same labyrinth that daily appeared before me.

Lucky you.

Such were the thoughts that occupied me during this time. Also I will admit that my mind turned often towards home and my parents and I wondered if word of my capture had yet reached them. If so my heart was heavy with the thought of how they would bear the news. It was sure to hit them like a cascade of stones and possibly crush them just as thoroughly. For they are old indeed by now and unused to such heavy blows. I admit I was never a perfect son but I like to think that I had brought them more joy than pain during my span of years in this world.

After some time we arrived at Gaza. Two weeks on the trail had left me filthy and foul and sticky with heathen saliva but trust the infidels to be oblivious of such things. I had lost much weight as well though—tall as I was—I remained an imposing figure especially as compared to them.

The temple of Dagon was as I've said a commanding structure but I had few new impressions of it: my eyes were failing fast and had weakened still further in the harsh arid sun and dust of the journey. I had a sense of stone walls as tall as many men one atop the next and so thick it took several paces to pass beyond them. Statues of I suppose their gods ringed the outside. I wasn't surprised at the size of the thing having seen it when in Gaza before. Heathens are always trying to build temples on an ever more imposing scale for obvious reasons. Even a child can see that they're trying to make up for their deities' lack of reality with phony grandeur and false awe. I've noticed in my life that the less substance a man carries inside the more he will try to create on the outside to make up for it and so will wear ever finer clothes and live in ever grander mansions and buy his wife ever more expensive jewels and then he will talk about these things to ensure that you don't overlook them and he will mention often what they cost. And so it was with the infidels—their temples which were supposed to be monuments to the divine were really only hollow echoing shouts at nothingness. No doubt one day the temples will reach all the way to the sky itself like greedy hands plucking at the heavens and those shouts will be the emptiest of all.

I've mentioned that the great hall inside was as big as some villages I've seen. We passed through it and down a narrow damp staircase to an underground cell where I was chained and left for days. After that I was brought upstairs to the great hall where I was taunted and ridiculed before being brought downstairs again. This went on for quite some time and during this period I grew to recognize Meneth the ironic priest (though I didn't yet know his name) and the woman who brought my food. My eyesight failed further.

I will admit there were bleak moments in that cell when I wept for Dalila and the love I bore her (such as it was) and the

way she had used it against me like a spear. But those times
grew fewer and fewer and then dried up completely until I felt
nothing but the kind of dull anger you have towards a dog that
once bit you or a harlot who left you with a rash. She—like me
like you like all of us—had a role to play in the LORD's plan
and dignifying it as anything more would be an error. You may
as well hold a lion responsible for its appetite. Might as well say
the beach is a victim of the sea.

Dagon in the Flesh

In the great hall of Dagon a fire burns in a pit in the
center of the room and there are more statues on raised plinths
dotted about and tall thin windows and columns supporting a
deep balcony running along the three sides of the chamber
that face me. The room being so huge I could imagine it easily
containing ranks of perhaps forty people across and sixty deep.
The balcony itself could hold half that number again. Now
there is as I've mentioned a great deal of furniture and other
material taking up space so I don't think there will be quite
such a crowd to witness my downfall that Meneth has
promised—but even so the size of the mob that could poten-
tially squeeze inside here is formidable. Nor is this the only
thing of note about the hall: for what I took to be a roof of
wooden timbers withstood a fierce storm just the other night
when I was chained there and then the sound of the rain upon
it led me to think it was slate. *Heavy beyond belief that ceiling
must be* I thought to myself. Add to that the weight of the balcony and truly those columns must be under extraordinary
pressure.

And then I thought about that some more. But once again I get ahead of myself. For these details of the roof and the great crowd that is gathering here were unknown to me upon my first arriving at the temple and that's what I'm telling you about now.

Dominating the stage upon which I'm chained is an enormous statue of Dagon. He looks down upon the chamber from the rearmost corner of the hall and his head is so tall that his gaze even falls upon the balconies. He is man-shaped from the head down with the kind of short curly beard so beloved by Philistine artisans if they can be called such. Below the waist he takes the form of a fish but not of any fish I have seen before for it's a blocky kind of specimen that holds the man portion upright on its pedestal and it looks more like a column with many rows of UUU-shaped etchings upon it to represent I suppose scales—and then a Y-shaped split at the bottom representing the division of a tail. Despite its ungainly form I know it's supposed to be a fish-man so that's what I will say it is.

And yes to answer your unspoken question: They worship this lifeless thing. They bow down and pray to it and beseech favors and the men bring their ailing doddering parents while their women kiss its fishy tail in hopes of begetting sons and overall it's expected to work all manner of wonders. I can explain no more for it is behavior beyond my understanding. The only good thing about the whole arrangement is that the idol has been shunted to the rear corner of the stage so while I am here my back is turned to the monstrosity and I wouldn't want it any other way.

One day I was brought to this hall and chained and left. I expected to be mocked as usual and then returned to the cellar but this was not to be and for my part I was glad of it for this chamber is warm and the dungeons are clammy and I had developed a cough which slowly dried up as I stood in chains. Of course I grew exhausted and when I dozed I fell hard against the manacles which bit into my wrists and left me with first welts and then sores but over time those sores scabbed over and toughened into calluses and by now I hardly notice anymore that I sleep standing up like a horse. And so the course of my life has brought me to this one point where I'm standing and can go no more than a step in any direction and this is where you've found me.

That's my story up until now.

As for where I will go next I have only a faint notion but I will not speak of it yet for it's too early to discuss in detail and I don't know if it'll work anyway.

More Entertainments

For another ten days the Philistines keep me enchained for their amusement. I know it's ten days because the main topic of their conversation is how long I've been their prisoner. They are prone to saying things like—Praise Dagon! The infidel has been with us already for sixty days! and then—sixty-one days! and then—sixty-two days! and so forth. When they are not gloating over my humiliation they seem primarily interested in telling one another how long they themselves have been in this cursed place.

—Ho Nukl! When did you get here?

—Yesterday says Nukl or—Two days since or—Three days since or whatever. With so much talk of the days passing it's easy enough to keep track of my own.

—Did you bring your wife then Nukl?

—Wives children cousins in-laws girlfriends concubines slaves Nukl chuckles.—Brought them all and why not?

—That's the truth isnit. Events like this don't happen every day. All praise to Dagon!

—Say that again growls Nukl and suddenly his voice drops and grows thick like burnt sugar.—For surely it's he who's delivered this heathen reptile into our hands as punishment for killing so many and destroying our country.

—So it is says the other voice all false piety and self-righteous grease. Then quieter as if turning to face me with a thoughtful look:—So it is.

Let them talk. I don't mind. I won't be leaving this pit of Hell alive and I'm at peace with that. But neither will they. Neither will they of this I'm certain. Each extra day of torment is a further surety of my plans which grow stronger and more inflexible like bricks hardening in the oven of my resolve. Every moment of their gloating is one moment struck from the futile course of their meaningless lives. And the irony is that they don't know it—they think it's my life that's futile & limited meaningless & doomed. But they will learn otherwise and their schooling shall be harsh and merciless.

The crowd has grown large enough that there is always a sizeable mob of bored and listless bullies with nothing to do but seek some diversion in alcohol or sex or me. Sometimes all three at once. I hear their chittering like a flock of crows bouncing around the stone-walled chamber or bats screeching in a cavern. Their boredom swirls with me at its center and the calls come forth for me to play or dance or entertain them in some way. At times I feel a woman's backside brush my crotch and their howling at my loins' response is especially lurid. Other times they force wine into my throat or braid flowers into my hair—which has now grown long enough for this—or go back to their old game of prodding me into dancing. I'm by now so strong that their prods and pokes barely trouble me but I don't want anyone to notice how much I've recovered so I go along and droop my head to let them think I'm troubled by their attentions. Swaying from side to side in a desultory way is enough to send them into gales of delight before they stagger off in search of more wine or harlots or both. Soon enough another gang appears and the whole nonsense is repeated.

I don't know what's become of Meneth who once put a stop to all this but who fails to do so now. Maybe he's praying to Dagon or maybe he's decided the mob will have its fun so there's no use fighting it.

There might I suppose be some coolheaded and sober types—some respectable elders or chaste women or clear-eyed children—but if so they fail to make themselves known. As ever it is the bullies and loudmouths who seize one's attention. From what I've seen in the course of my life the Philistines are in no wise unique in this.

The other thing that delights the rabble is to talk of Dalila's ploy in bringing me to heel. Long days I spend listening to their tales growing ever more convoluted and embroidered. One fool swears that Dalila was no Philistine at all but a turncoat Israelite who took revenge on her people following her rape by a half dozen of her fellow villagers. Others maintain that Dalila was actually three women or four or six and that they subdued me through main force or that I submitted to them willingly in exchange for promises of sex and humiliation. Another says that Dalila's reward for betraying me was a retinue of a hundred thick-loined slaves from all over the provinces and Goshen besides and that she has her own palace in Sorec where she is pleasured all day long and young men wait outside the gates to beg their chance to go inside and lie with her. There's no choice but to listen to the drivel so listen I do and through it all I manage to discern kernels of truth about events that occurred when I wasn't present—at such times as when Dalila met with the Philistine princes. These I have conveyed in the telling of my story as I've seen fit. Doubtful it is that these speakers were present any more than I was but stories have a way of getting around from one person to the next and they have to begin somewhere. So it is that I learn of the price paid for my abduction and of the princes' growing agitation as attempt after attempt to capture me failed and pressure upon Dalila was increased and much else. As I digest it all any soft feelings I may have harbored for Dalila even in retrospect grow cold and withered and calloused and dead and that's as it should be. I don't allow myself the luxury of hatred for even that is a kind of passion isn't it? And I won't admit any such towards her even in the guise of fury.

What remains as I said already is the respect felt by a defeated warrior for the commander who humbled him. But this is far from love or passion kindness or goodwill of any sort.

All the while more and still more infidels arrive. There must be thousands by now. I've heard from the gossip that some large event has been planned by the priests for two days hence. The grand finale as it were. I need hardly wonder what it will entail. I only wonder whether I will have the strength to defy it.

The Final Insult

The next day Meneth visits me. For a long time I don't know it's him: I know only that someone has chased off the hooligans and is standing beside me for some length of time. I wonder who it is and then have an idea.—Come to gloat have you Dalila?

A quiet snuffling laugh then but it's a male voice that answers.—Dalila is far from here Meneth says.—She's gone back home last I heard.

—More whoring I suppose? Despite myself I can't keep the anger from my voice and I'm almost surprised to hear it.

—Hardly says Meneth.—She's quite the hero you know. You should hear how people speak of her. I doubt there's ever been a harlot so highly regarded in the history of the world.

—I know what they're saying I snapped.—I hear it every day.

Meneth's shrug is almost audible.—As you like. You mentioned her name so I thought to tell you. She is settled back home and doing well. She's a rich woman now you know. Rumors are she's even married but I don't know whether that's true. In any case it's not my intent to trouble you.

—You flatter yourself. You couldn't trouble me if you tried. But despite my brave words my hands have clenched and my newly grown fingernails stab my palms.

—Hmm yes. Well I shan't argue with you this being your ahh final day of existence.

I say nothing. This isn't such a shock since as I said I've been catching the gossip.

Meneth goes on—Tomorrow morning the priests will make an offering to Dagon and the other gods to give thanks for your capture. This will take most of the morning and won't be public. At midday they will convene here in front of anyone who wants to watch and will cut out your heart and drain it into a basin and will drink of your blood. This too will be made available to anyone who wants a sip.

He pauses.—There are three thousand people here. The priests don't expect much of your blood to be left at the conclusion of the ceremony.

—If you're trying to scare me I tell him—you're failing. What awaits you and your priests in the next life is far worse than some barbarian in this one.

—I'm not trying to scare you he says.—At least such is not my sole purpose.

—Then why are you here wasting my time and your breath?

He sighs or seems to.—Wasting my breath he says—yes that's what it feels like. But I've little choice in the matter. I'm a priest of Dagon and I have duties after all.

—What duties are those? I sneer.—To torment your victims to rub their wounds with gravel and salt and—what did you say—drink their blood? Some priest you are. I spit at him where I think he stands. Hope he stands.

He is silent a time. Then he says—Actually I had hoped you would come to your senses and convert.

The Last Surprise

Anyone seeking evidence of Philistine lunacy need look no further than this.

—Are you mad? I say finally. This is long after Meneth has spoken: I'm so startled that it takes some while to understand what he's said and that he's serious.—Or maybe I add after a time—you intend a joke at your prisoner's expense.

—I never joke about Dagon Meneth says quietly.

—Well I do I snap.

Meneth exhales with a kind of grunt as if it pains him to even stand here with me.—Listen he says.—Your people go on about your god and how he's chosen your people above all others to receive his message and carry it. From Abram right through Moses and Josue and all the rest you've made it clear that divinity is a special part of your birthright. He gave you Moses to lead you through the desert and Josue to raze the walls and destroy the cities and claim the land—

—*Re*claim I say loudly.

—and all the while your Yahweh is up in the sky making sure you come out on top. Except of course—and here he pauses like a storyteller in a crowded market—when you lose.

—The facts speak for themselves I say.—What's your point?

—My point is it's all rubbish. What kind of deity creates the world only to inject strife into it? Favors one tribe over another and then sets them at war? It makes no sense. It's beyond comprehension.

—Beyond *your* comprehension I reply fighting to keep my voice calm but I feel my muscles tense and the chains that bind them grow taut.—Perhaps you confuse your intellect with God's and mistake your lack of understanding for a shortcoming on His part.

Meneth pauses as if considering this. Then he says.—No I don't think so.

His calm infuriates me. I know it shouldn't but I'm a man prone to sudden furious outbursts and such habits aren't to be forgotten in a day.—I suppose your Dagon loves all men I sneer at him.—I suppose he loves his enemies and forgives them their sins and welcomes them all into an afterlife dripping with honey and cream.

His reply takes so long to come I wonder if he's walked away.—No not that he says finally.—Dagon loves only those who love him and he hates all others and will not hesitate to consign them to oblivion.

—So then I say.—Your god is as irrational as you say mine is.

—Not at all he says—for Dagon will welcome any man into his flock. A man's lineage is unimportant. That's why I've come here so you can taste of his mercy and place yourself in his care.

I tell him—I would sooner vomit blood.

—You may ahh get your wish he says.—Let me lay it out as clearly as possible. Continue to proclaim your inane claptrap about how your particular tribe is favored by the creator of the universe—I believe you claim him to be the sole creator isn't that so?—and tomorrow you'll die a painful and humiliating death.

—That means nothing to me.

—Perhaps not but it might mean something to your god. Imagine how he will look if his own champion here on earth is allowed to be executed and ahh consumed by his greatest enemies. Hmm? Not good I shouldn't think. Not good at all.

In my mind I begin reciting lineages to keep his insinuating words at bay. *Adam begat Seth who begat Enos. Enos begat Cainan who begat Melaleel who begat—Henoch? No—it was Jared. Who then begat Henoch . . .*

—On the other hand he pushes on—suppose you were to publicly renounce this provincial deity of yours and place yourself under the protective wing of Dagon. Several things would happen very quickly. First of all your treatment here would immediately improve. Better food certainly and a private cell as well. A few weeks of preaching about the unmatched power of Dagon and how he is mightier than all the other gods of the earth and you'd be allowed a degree of freedom. And in six months who knows? Pledge yourself a priest and take a few Philistine wives and in all likelihood you could walk out of this temple a free man. Believe me that doesn't happen often.

He pauses.—And oh yes we wouldn't kill you tomorrow or drink your blood. That's something to consider.

Sweat is pooling around my eyes but I can't wipe it. *And Mathusala begat Lamech . . .* It is the sweat of rage.—And you really think I would do this just to save myself?

—Save yourself? Oh no I don't think that. But you might do it to save your god hmm?

I'm baffled so I say nothing. He explains—You see Samson if we kill you then we kill your god. We drink his blood tomorrow and piss it away the next day and let's face it there's nothing less frightening than a god who has been reduced to piss and shit. But if you renounce Yahweh well that's a victory for us—quite a nice one—but the worst thing that happens to your god is that he's laughed at for a time and then forgotten. He becomes irrelevant but better to be irrelevant than to be piss and shit. Don't you agree?

—My people will denounce me as a traitor. You'd like that wouldn't you?

—Let them say what they want. Your people aren't here. They'll denounce you as a failure whatever happens but at least this way they can go on believing what they want. No harm done to ahh I believe it's Yahweh isn't it?

Despite myself I listen to his words and answer them.—You needn't concern yourself about harming Him.

—Yes but. As I explained—your death would do the kind of irrevocable damage that your renunciation would not. With you here as a priest of Dagon your little tribe can carry on with its quaint customs unmolested—though frankly that tribe is just about ready to drop out of the world's memory and it can take Yahweh with it. No one will notice he's gone. Meanwhile Dagon's glory is augmented and you retain your life. You see? Everyone benefits.

—You lying cur I say quietly.—For me to renounce the One True God would be a blow more damning than my own death. Better by far that I die and you know it.

I'm breathing so hard I can barely talk so I say no more. Meneth murmurs like a snake:—If that's what you think ahh well—far be it from me to make any effort to dissuade you.

—It's the truth I manage to growl—as you well know.

Despite his promises he stays on for a time to whisper more oily platitudes in my ear. I hear them not. *Lamech begat Noe who begat three sons named Sem Cham and Japheth.* I ignore Meneth's lies and remind myself that the serpent tempted Eve with cunning words and also that Dalila used them to break me down. Words are the enemy. They form themselves into arguments that twist themselves into doubts that wriggle into a man's stomach and grow bigger like a woman carrying a child. It occurs to me that maybe this is why women are less prone to doubts than men: because they have no room inside to carry them being taken up as they are with the mechanisms of childbearing. In some ways their minds are set on more practical things as a result. And I get so distracted with this idea even now on the eve of my death that Meneth grows tired of my unresponsiveness and strides off in disgust.

A Visitation in the Night

That night I awaken to a temple heavy in the midst of slumber. The hall is filled with the musk of sleeping bodies—hundreds of them snoring & farting murmuring & breathing. Dull nightsounds coddle me but even so I know I'm not alone.—Who's there? I say.

—No one you know comes the answer.—A visitor.

—Come to mock me?

—No. Just to see.

The voice is dry and leathery and I imagine an old woman bent low. Wizened cheeks like river valleys and thick rheumatic fingers and dusty robes much worn. I ask her—What's your name?

—My name isn't important.

Part of me is annoyed to be awakened but part is curious too.—What do you want then?

—I want to understand you who have done such evil she says. Mockery indeed.—Begone I spit.

Instead she says—Tell me what you have done with your life.

—I've striven to give glory to the name of Yahweh I answer.

—And how did you do this?

—By slaying His enemies. By showing that none could withstand His awesome glory. By burning their fields and leaving their widows to grieve and their children to starve.

The old woman pauses as if considering.—And you did this for Him?

—Of course.

—Not for yourself?

For a moment I feel that dreamlike confusion that arises from everyday expectations gone awry.—What do you mean?

—I mean your enemies claim that you sought glory for your name not your god's. That you enjoy violence for its own sake because you're too stupid to win an argument through clear reasoning. That you are motivated by fear & hatred pettiness & savagery not to mention lust wrath envy greed and even a certain gluttony for violence and above all pride—the mother of the entire brood—and that these were the motivations that burned within you.

—Unfair! I thrash.—Is there nothing they won't accuse me of?

—Well she says.—No one has mentioned sloth.

—Believe not a word! I cry and then realize that raising my voice at this dark hour is bound to bring unwelcome attention.—I'm not a perfect man I admit. A simple son of my people is all I claim to be. But know this: when I acted I acted in the LORD's interests and against the LORD's enemies. When I slew them it was His strength that guided my arm and His hunger that filled my belly. Do you know that on my wedding night I killed thirty men?

—I've heard as much she says softly.—Those men would live today if not for you.

—If not for the LORD I correct her.—Any strength I enjoy comes from Him. So ignore the lies of small bitter men who lead small bitter lives. They will enjoy small bitter deaths and nothing else.

—Is that right? whispers the crone.

From her tone I can tell she understands nothing and I say as much. Then I am privy to a long exhalation—a sigh as it were from her very soul. This crippled heathen then has the nerve to tell me—That's where you're wrong. I understand you perfectly.

I don't bother to answer and soon afterwards drop off again into sleep. Whether she stays beside me or leaves I neither know nor care. When I awaken much later I'm alone.

The Manner of My Execution

The day I am to die dawns quietly. I lift my head to early-morning sounds of infidels rousing themselves in the temple all around me. The air is filled with expectation or so it seems to me. Maybe every man who knows the appointed moment of his death feels the same: that his last morning is unique in the history of the world and of particular concern to all who are yet living. Moreover that it carries a hush a stillness a sense of anticipation that sets it apart from all other days.

I don't know if other condemned men feel this. It would be something to find out.

Unlike other mornings there is little rowdiness or carrying on. It's as if the dawn has delivered some somber change and everyone behaves accordingly. Voices are muted and nobody comes to harass me. This muted quality is present for a long time and then at some point an unfamiliar buzzing hum can be noticed echoing across the great hall. Slowly it grows louder and more noticeable. It's the kind of sound you realize you've already been hearing for some while without remarking but once it registers you can think of nothing else. Gradually the murmuring of the people in the hall vanishes altogether. The quiet of consternation fills the chamber as the hum grows louder and brings with it a hollow quality as can be heard when you stand a distance from the sea with a row of dunes intervening.

There is also a rhythm to the sound: whuh-*whuh* whuh-*whuh* whuh-*whuh* whuh-*whuh*

The stone walls of the room bounce the sound about so it layers upon itself and grows thick. Around me people are whispering. I can't make out their words but it's obvious what they're asking about.

Then I hear a woman's clear voice say—It's the priests. They're praying.

She is right. I can imagine it easily enough: ranks of priests in some incense-filled chamber nearby with their heads bowed or on their knees or perhaps flat on their bellies. Wearing black-dyed robes or crimson or maybe purple. Maybe they're naked who knows? and hunkered nose to anus. Whatever Dagon likes. Whatever they imagine Dagon likes. There must be a lot of them since they make the kind of noise that can only come from a large number of throats simultaneously and then the sound has to travel through thick walls. Block upon block of stone. Who knows what the priests are saying—some drivel most likely.

Dagon oh *lord* we *wor*ship *you* now *hear* our *prayers* we *send* to *thee*

Or being heathens Philistines and fools they're just as likely mouthing whuh-*whuh* whuh-*whuh* whuh-*whuh* whuh-*whuh* and thinking they're putting in a good day's work.

The thought makes me smile and in the tense air of the chamber this doesn't go unnoticed.

—Look at him now says a quiet voice off to my left.—Dead by midday and he's standin there gigglin.

—Off his head I don't guess says another.

The voices are quiet not taunting. They're talking to each other about me not to me directly for entertainment's sake. The second voice goes on—Can you blame him though after being strung up so long?

—I can blame him for anythin I want says the first voice—includin what he did to us before we brought him here.

—Point says the other.—You gotta point.

There is a pause as they I imagine study me.

—Gotta say though says the second voice.—For all that he's been strung up all this time he don't look half bad does he?

—He looks like dog shit says the first.—He looks like a bitch.

Now this *is* for my benefit.

Whuh-*whuh* whuh-*whuh* whuh-*whuh* whuh-*whuh* whuh-*whuh* whuh-*whuh* whuh-*whuh*

—When he's dead I'll dance the voice continues.—I'll stay up all night drinkin and dancin and won't go to sleep till the sun's up.

The second man laughs quietly as they slink away.—You'll have company for the drink my friend but you'll have to dance for the both of us. Gotta admit though. He ain't lookin too shabby for a guy's been through what he has. . . .

The infidel is right about this: I feel better than I have in months. Arms throbbing with power—back suffering not an ache or twinge nor my neck either. Legs feel strong enough to carry me through the desert for forty days if so called upon and lungs as well. Energy buzzes through my veins and I know the LORD is with me again. Not that He ever left but He's smiling upon me once more and giving me strength and it's only now that I realize how much I've been missing that. I feel my tongue strong in my mouth. My hair tumbles halfway down my back. My loins rest like iron against my thigh. Even my hearing seems supernaturally charged and part of me half wonders if my sight is to be returned as well. But I know better than to question the LORD's design. If He wants me to see then I will see and if not then it means blindness will be no more of an obstacle than a missing sense of taste or smell or pain.

A skeptic would say that I'm merely imbued with the strength of fear—the final hysteria that rises up in a man who knows he's to die. Sounds are sharper air is sweeter memories are more vivid when you know you'll soon leave them forever. So say the unbelievers: but I know better.

Whuh-*whuh* whuh-*whuh* whuh-*whuh* whuh-*whuh* whuh-*whuh* whuh-*whuh* whuh-*whuh*

At the beginning of this history I told you that I would start it and end it in chains and so I have. But I also said it would get worse before it was through and maybe in your mind that's true as well. But to me just the opposite has happened. My newly returned power is a harbinger a sign an omen and though I'm not much of one to pay attention to such things this time I'm helpless to ignore it. As are my enemies I might add. They will get a taste soon enough.

Soon enough.

For I must admit: until this moment I've been unsure as to whether my plan would work but now I doubt no longer. The LORD would not go to the trouble of gifting me with such powers as I now have if He didn't intend for me to use them and He wouldn't intend *that* if He didn't mean for them to work. Well do I know that sometimes the LORD's plans and my own are not an exact match but I know too that whatever

He has in mind will be if not equal to my own hopes then something that will far surpass them.

Whuh-*whuh* whuh-*whuh* whuh-*whuh* whuh-*whuh* whuh-*whuh* whuh-*whuh* whuh-*whuh*

The morning passes. The chanting grows in intensity and after a time I get a headache with it. Then as midday approaches the pain recedes as if to remind me that all things both good and bad are transient.

Whuh-*whuh* whuh-*whuh* whuh-*whuh* whuh-*whuh* whuh-*whuh* whuh-*whuh* whuh-*whuh*

The chanting grows louder yet and more frantic. Occasional shrieks punctuate its steady rhythm like the cackling of unpleasant birds.

This doesn't go unobserved by the increasingly restless guests in the great hall.

Whuh-*whuh*whuh*whuh*kaiiiwhuh*whuh*whuhkaiiiyahhh-whuh*whuh*huh*whuh*whuhaiii*whuh*

—Sounds like they gettin worked up in there. If I hadda guess I'd be thinkin it's time fer the big display pretty soon.

—Might be right bout that. Jus wish they'd get on wit it.

As it turns out we don't have long to wait.

Whuh*whuh*whuh*whuh*whuh*whuh*whuh*whuh*whuh*whuh* whuh*whuh*whuhwhuhwhuh*

A silence.

Whuh.

Another one.

WHUH!

The chanting ceases. It's like hearing your heart stop beating. Its absence is so sudden and so complete that for a moment I feel dizzy.

A hush falls across the hall that lasts a long time as if in the sudden silence nobody wants to be the first one to make a sound. People even breathe carefully so as not to attract attention. Then there's a great rumpus at the far end of the hall—I suppose it's not such a big noise but in this air of expectation it sounds like a mountain cracking asunder—as a pair of heavy doors swing open. And such a creaking and groaning they make they must be some massive slabs too. Then the shuffling of countless pairs of feet and I imagine the priests walking into the hall their faces no doubt grave and self-important as only a heathen can be when he's praying to his lifeless god. Other things I hear besides and some of them puzzle me like the clink of chains and I wonder if other victims are to be sacrificed along with me or maybe before me as some sort of minor ritual before the main one but this I never learn. Also at irregular intervals come various loud reports as if hard wood mallets are being slapped against the backs or thighs of some unfortunates but again I never learn for sure what this is. Maybe they're hitting one another or even themselves. Madness I know it sounds like but I think I've established that with heathen priests lunacy is no bar to devotion.

One thing I'm sure of: the sound is moving towards me. I imagine some sort of procession with the priests at the van of it and the guests jammed up alongside and also stuffed into the balcony that I've described running along three sides of the place. Come to think of it the rich and influential would be more likely to have their seats up above where the viewing is good rather than crammed in below with the rabble. So in my mind's eye that's how I picture it: a thick column of priests in the middle of the hall—pompous in robes dyed white or black, for those seem to be the colors favored by priests of any

persuasion—holding smoking tapers and smeared with the
noxious perfume that chokes me even at this distance. Incense
too filling the room with a thin haze. Behind them and on each
side the mob packed in trying to get a good look at what's going on yet at the same time trying not to push overmuch lest
they appear disrespectful. Not that such concerns will hold any
of them back for long for it's tough to keep up such pretense
especially for a heathen and especially once the knives come
out. Overhead hangs the deep wooden balcony with its ornate
screenwork and railings where the elite and those who think
they are sit in their bright-colored clothes like so many stoic
birds. Showing their good breeding with their silence and re-
straint but believe me if I let them cut my throat that flock will
grow raucous enough.

The procession stops. For a time the only sound in the great
hall is the crackle of tapers and the occasional cough quickly
hushed as some poor soul chokes on the incense smoke. The
scene is so weighty it's nearly comical. I almost laugh. Almost.

Then a priest's deep voice intones—To whom do we owe life?

And with one voice the assembled mob roars—Dagon!

—And to whom do we owe this day?

—Dagon!

—To whom do we show our faith?

—*Dagon!*

—Yahweh! I shout back but no one is bothered. A moment
later I feel stupid for my outburst. It proved nothing: my views
on the subject are already known so all it did was point up my
own helplessness.

The priest's voice is deep and strong but somehow bovine
too like a dull-witted cow's. He says—This day we shall repay
Dagon for the gift he has delivered unto us.

The crowd shuffles and stirs.

—When this villain is slain and his blood is drunk the priest goes on—we shall be rid of him and his tribe and their meddlesome god for all time.

—Har! cry out some and—Yes! and—Dagon is merciful!

How much more of this I can bear without retching I know not. Fortunately as it turns out not much more is forthcoming. It seems the priests have used up their supply of patience with all their whuh-whuh-*whuh*ing and now they're eager to wallow in shit and blood. So the next thing I feel is a pair of hands groping along my manacles turning first this latch and then that and then my arms are free and I let them flop weakly to my sides because I know that is what the crowd expects and then I realize I should appear weaker than this so I totter on my feet as if swooning before collapsing onto the stone floor. It's all nonsense of course—I've rarely felt stronger in my life and my blood thrums with the touch of the LORD's fingers but it would do no good to let my enemies see that now. So I fall and let myself land heavily against the granite.

The rabble is suitably pleased.—Weak as a baby! trills one woman while another says—Slice his throat now before he gets up.

—That's right calls another.—Show him the same mercy he showed us!

The priest is quick to put a stop to that.—Pick him up he commands—and bring him to the rear of the altar.

My mind is moving quickly trying to picture where I am. Before my eyes failed I studied the place as best I could but now that I'm free and blind everything seems bigger and more disorienting. The part of the altar that's been behind me I glimpsed only briefly while enchained. I know the statue of Dagon stands to one side and there is a pair of columns supporting this end of the roof. Beyond that I can say nothing for sure.

My plan is quickly falling to pieces. I had thought to yank on the chains that bound me—trying to tear out the columns that held them—but I realize now that the iron is far weaker than the stone and would snap uselessly. And then I would be faced with three thousand enemies I can't see and even with the spirit of the LORD upon me would I have a hard time of it indeed trying to slay that many unseen foes before making my way stumbling and tripping from the temple into the wider world.

Then there is the question of what I would do once outside. Even supposing I made my way through the city of Gaza and safely to my people's territory then what? Live like a cripple— an invalid to be doted upon? A man in the prime of his life such as myself whose history is spelled out in blood and fire can't change his ways so quickly to write the remainder of his life story with the alphabet of charity and pity. Call me proud for I've been called worse things but I would rather not live at all than live like that.

My mind spins like a grinding wheel to find a new plan for I can't believe I've been left here for so long for no reason. And my hair grown back too. Surely the LORD must have a purpose for me if only I can spy it.

The priest says—Take him to the rear of the altar and hold him there.

My thoughts grope like a blind man. There are columns back there. Unlike those that I've been chained to these pillars stand hard by each other and if anything are more massive.

Maybe they're so important to the balance of the structure that if they were to topple they'd take some of the main temple building with them. Maybe not. But maybe so.

My hope settles upon this idea like a hornet on the butt end of a mule.

—Hold him? says one of my escorts. A boy judging from the sound of his voice.

—Yes hold him says the priest.—Hold him up can't you see how weak he is? Dagon has punished him for his sins and now he can hardly stand.

As if to prove the fool right I stumble heavily nearly toppling the boy as I do so. The other grabs at my arm.—Please I murmur into the boy's ear.—Let me lean into something. Aren't there two pillars at the rear of the altar?

—Save it the boy hisses.—I'm not here to do your bidding.

—You're in no condition to make demands adds the other.

—Let me stand against the columns I gasp.—I'm not demanding I'm begging. Believe me there's few men alive who can claim they've heard Samson do that.

Maybe this nourishes the lads' pride. For whatever reason they do as I ask and while the priests continue to quietly intone some rubbish to the majestic grandeur of Dagon the two boys lead me by the arms to the pillars. They're enormous things so wide that the curve of them is barely noticeable: if I had come up against them alone I'd've thought they were merely sections of the wall or a short hallway slightly canted out of true.

—Here we are the boys tell me.

Where the two columns stand next to each other there's a nook something like a doorway. Imagine two huge pillars each one ten cubits across with enough space between for a man to stand with his hands held close up beside his shoulders.

—That's far enough snaps one of my escorts.—There's no use trying to hide back there. You'd get caught soon enough. Stand out here and face your fate like a man.

A boy is telling me this. A child. I choke back a laugh and then think *Why am I doing that?* so I laugh full in his face. As the echoes die away I realize the priests have stopped blathering and the hall has gone silent. Doubtless they've all seen me laughing at this pup. Well good I say. And seeing as how I have their attention I cry out—Witness now the power of Yahweh!

A voice—maybe Meneth's—replies blandly—We've been observing it for some months.

A good reply I must admit but also the last he will ever make. I set my shoulders and lean forward slightly with my palms pressing flat against the columns to either side. The stone is so strong I think I might weep but I remember the LORD and stiffen my resolve. Beside me I sense my escorts shifting uncertainly as if wondering what I'm up to. No doubt the priests and mob are wondering too. A murmur rumbles through the crowd but nobody's scared as yet.

Fools.

Power skitters through my arms like ants. I've no doubts that I can accomplish what I need to do but it'll take some effort: it won't happen just like that. Waves of strength are building up in me—pounding through my sinews like surf against the rocks—but I need time. To distract the crowd from understanding what they're seeing I shout—So I hear there are a thousand of you come to watch me die. Is that true?

A huge roar goes up at that just as I had hoped. Of course there are more than a thousand and every idiot there wants to be the one to tell me so. While they carry on I shift the weight from my hips into my back and from my back into my shoulders and from my shoulders into my biceps and I push. I push.

And nothing happens.

—Three thousand! jeers the mob.—There's more than three thousand come to watch you perish.

So then. Three thousand heathens will die when this building comes crashing to earth. And such horror will fill their hearts as they will never forget.

I hang my head as if in despair at their words but really I'm putting my head down so as to throw more weight into my arms but still nothing is happening and for an awful moment I wonder if I've misunderstood the LORD's plans and confused them with my own and then I wonder if it's my destiny after all to die here with my throat slit and my blood coursing through the veins of three thousand unbelievers.

And even as I think this I feel the faintest trickle of something giving way. It might be the column shifting just so slightly on its base or it could be my shoulder grinding against its socket. Frankly at this point I'm unable to tell.

Still the crowd howls on. The priests are trying to hush them up but for the moment they've lost control of the cacophony which suits me fine.

Beneath my right hand the column murmurs and shifts. It's unmistakable this time.

I should explain something about these columns. There are different ways to build them using different kinds of stone. These are granite and the thing to remember about granite is that it's heavy beyond comprehension and backbreaking for men to haul. So when it's quarried out the stonecutters hack it into pieces roughly cube-shaped and then shave it down further into fat thick circles so as to transport no more than is absolutely necessary. These segments are hauled on skids or sleds or rollers or some such—to be honest I've never bothered to find out—and then they're stacked up with levers and pulleys and great numbers of men sweating in their labor. So pillars such as these as tall as ten men are made of enormous slabs of stone stacked in layers. First they're piled up then straightened out then smoothed down and polished to look like one big tower. Sometimes you may see a sheath of gold or marble added to hide the seams but the Philistines not being known for their refinement are not in the habit of doing this.

So when I say I feel the stone shift under my palm you shouldn't think that I'm pushing the whole towering mass away from me. Rather it's as if I'm pushing against a stack of crates and the bottommost one is being knocked out of kilter. As I learned long ago—when a few burning foxes started a war that left thousands dead—it takes only a modest disruption to create an inordinate amount of chaos. That's what I'm trying to do right now: create a small disruption and a temple full of havoc at the same time.

Then beneath my left hand the column gives way the tiniest fraction.

The priests have succeeded in shouting down the mob and now they're haranguing me. I don't know if anyone's figured out what I'm up to but even if they have there's no man alive who could wrench my arms away from this stone. Where the two boys have gone who escorted me here I don't know. If they're smart they've left but I've no reason to think they're smart. Certainly from all the hisses & catcalls jeers & loud priestly orations it doesn't seem anyone else has gotten the message and run away.

—Kill him! someone shrieks from the crowd. A woman it

sounds like and I entertain the fleeting thought that whoever said women were less bloodthirsty than men was either lying or profoundly unschooled in the ways of the world.

—That bastard murdered my family hollers another voice.—Cut his throat!

The column to my left shifts another fraction. Slower to get started it now moves more easily than the other.

—Brothers says a voice that can only be a priest's.—And sisters too! Let us retain our dignity before Dagon. This is a day that should bring glory to him not ignominy to his followers.

The voice is familiar. I wonder if it's Meneth's again or if my ears are fooled by the prattle that all priests seem partial to.

Beneath my left hand the column suddenly gives way nearly the width of my finger. An ominous scraping reverberates through the chamber.

—Eh? says the Meneth-maybe-priest.—What was that?

—The prisoner! cries another.—He is snuffling in fear! See how he cowers there.

—Cry all you want hollers yet a third.—It won't help you.

If that's what they think—fine. I breathe deep filling my lungs with not just air but also strength & resolve certainty & the LORD's grace. With my eyes screwed shut tight I heave mightily against both columns at once: my arms strain to open like an angel's wings caught in the grip of Satan. Sweat runnels down my back and alongside my nose and under my arms: my hands are slippery with it but the cool smooth stone sucks away the moisture and won't let me lose my grip. I sense some consternation in the crowd but this is only a distraction and I won't let distractions get the better of me so I squeeze my eyes even tighter—not that this matters given the state of my vision—and empty my mind so as to have a conversation with the stone.

Hello my friends I think to the columns. *I ask a favor of you.*

We promise nothing the stone whispers back. *But it never hurts to ask.*

This might. This might hurt a lot.

The stone says nothing but only shifts another finger width beneath my efforts.

Ah! I whisper soundlessly. *You know what I want already. I need you to move for me. To give way and tumble and collapse and let the whole structure above come crashing down.*

There is a pause as the stones consider and nothing much happens. Finally the stone says: *To be sure this is a strange request.*

To be sure I gasp.

No one has ever asked such a thing before. In fact the requests we hear are usually for just the opposite—to stand upright & strong reliable & true.

I'm sure that's so. This is however a special case.

Well then. We must think on this for a time.

Think not too long I beg you. For my enemies and those of the LORD are poised to strike me down and humiliate the One True God and they plan to do so even now in this hall in which you stand. And so you are faced with a choice: either to let it happen and be remembered only for this infamy or to prevent it from happening and be remembered as the means by which the infidels were slaughtered and Samson was avenged and the glory of the LORD made plain unto all the world.

The stone hesitates only a moment. *You should have said so in the first place.*

Didn't think of it I admit.

Ah well. No harm done.

And with that the stone beneath my fingers shears away and my arms straighten suddenly and I fall forward onto the hard stone floor. My chin splits against the unforgiving surface and I roll on my back and an amazing thing happens: my vision is restored. Not entirely but enough for me to make out the tableau around me. And although I am doomed to die in moments yet do I know that this is a scene I will never forget.

How I Exit the World

For a terrible moment the columns teeter overhead as if held in place by diabolical threads. Their bases have skated away by the power of my arms and now the stone pillars lean into each other like drunkards or lovers. But not for long that much is obvious. They tilt overhead and look down at us tiny mortals and I am reminded not for the first time of my insignificance in the eyes of the LORD.

The statue of Dagon stands unmoving with its back to the danger. As if dull and dumb and unaware which is of course the truth.

But the mob crushing into the chamber is aware and a great scream rises up from them like a flock of birds taking wing. The mighty howling of three thousand souls doomed and damned and realizing all together that their lives are about to end with the merest brush of the One True God's fingertips. And what a pretty song it is too. That rushing howl ascending against the columns as if to hold them off and beat them back but such is not possible as the sound hasn't yet been heard that can push away stone. The columns tumble earthward in a slow dreamy taking-their-time kind of way but when they land it is with such a loud crack it's as if twin thunderbolts have lashed the chamber.

Dozens of Philistines are instantly smashed to puddles but many more rush away. All in vain however as great clouds of stone chips lash into the crowd: the columns shatter on impact and hundreds of heathens are pitted through with projectiles as if the LORD has chosen to righteously stone every sinner at once. It is a hailstorm of rock: it is a cloudburst of annihilation. The mob is shot through and sprayed with scarlet and the very stone runs red with death.

The statue of Dagon totters.

I hear further keening from overhead and raise my miraculously restored eyes to the balconies where the most elite part of the crowd has crammed itself in to watch my execution. That event is far from their minds at the moment. Right now they are surging back and forth like a school of terrified fish pushing and jostling and fighting to flee the building before the stone temple comes crashing entirely down upon them. They're in such a panic that their efforts are causing the very balcony to sag and judder beneath their feet. Then I realize it's not the crowd causing the balcony to sway but rather its supporting pillars which are heaving unsteadily now that I've knocked over the first two. Some fluke of the way the building's weight is distributed has got the rest of the columns rocking back and forth as if arguing among themselves whether to continue with their labor or else simply give up and fall. The heavy roof of course is a factor in all this as well.

An unholy screech pulls my attention back to the stage. The statue of Dagon—never the most artistic or well balanced of creations—has been knocked askew by a chunk of tumbling stone and sent reeling as if slapped. Even as I watch it whirls with indescribable slowness as if uncertain whether to stand or fall—stand or fall—regain its balance or topple into the crowd. At length the tired old idol makes up his mind and spins almost gracefully into the nearest pillar. Unlike my efforts the statue disjoints not the bottom of the column but the top—raining down unfathomably massive blocks of stone onto the waiting worshippers. Their cries are loud but brief. And then the statue and the column fall full length into the next column which shudders and trembles and cracks and falls full length into the next one and so on.

The end comes quickly after that and I don't see everything. One by one the columns ringing the hall snap and shatter and tumble to the ground leaving the next in line to bear even more of the temple's weight. Of course none of them can so the next one shatters even faster than the one before and so on. It reminds me of the child's game in which small rectangles of wood are set up on edge in a long line and then the first is knocked into the next causing the whole line of them to totter and collapse. When half the columns are gone the balcony dislodges with a great crunching sound and a shower of stone & brick mortar dust & bodies as the heathens are flung into empty space to fall upon their brethren who are already dead and broken beneath the clutter of granite and if any on the balcony survive the fall—which is few enough I don't doubt— then there's no question of whether they die in the ensuing collapse of the roof itself which clatters upon them in a roar of stone blocks and plaster chips.

I make no special exemption for myself for I am there in the midst of it as well and the roof crashing down at last upon the crowd will kill me—I know this—just as surely as any sinner.

When my eyes close and the last light of my life is snuffed to darkness like a room's final candle I am left with no more than a smile on my face and the knowledge that all of us are born with: that the day will come and sooner than we expect when our final blindness will arrive to remain with us for all eternity.

So it is with one last great effort that I lift my head and cry out these my final words:—My name is SAMSON and I have killed thousands for the LORD and so pleased Him mightily!

My life is a prayer that has come to its end.

Amen.

CPSIA information can be obtained at www.ICGtesting.com
Printed in the USA
BVOW071645120812

297641BV00001B/4/P